SHANNON

She was the darling of the town, the beautiful and spirited daughter of the man who ruled with an iron hand – until Shannon rode in. He was young and dangerous and mystery surrounded him like a cloak. For the rich man's daughter it was love at first sight. All agreed that nothing good could come of their relationship, but the young lovers were unaware of the menace hanging over their heads – and nobody could foresee that, before this murderous week was through, the town's very survival would depend on Shannon and his flaming gun.

SHANNON

SHANNON

by

Dempsey Clay

Dales Large Print Books
Long Preston, North Yorkshire,
BD23 4ND, England.

British Library Cataloguing in Publication Data.

Clay, Dempsey
    Shannon.

    A catalogue record of this book is
    available from the British Library

    ISBN   1-84262-330-3 pbk

First published in Great Britain in 2003 by Robert Hale Ltd.

Copyright © Dempsey Clay 2003

Cover illustration © Longaron by arrangement with
Norma Editorial S.A.

Published in Large Print 2004 by arrangement with
Robert Hale Ltd.

Dales Large Print is an imprint of Library Magna Books Ltd.

Printed and bound in Great Britain by
T.J. (International) Ltd., Cornwall, PL28 8RW

CHAPTER 1

ALONG CAME A STRANGER

The staccato beat of racing hoofs was muted in the vast stillness of the night before exploding abruptly into a storming crescendo of sound as the Bannerman gang erupted from the mouth of the steep walled arroyo to hit the sweep of alkali sloping down towards the Twelve Canyons country and the Sawteeth Divide.

A huge cloud of bitter dust welled up in a rolling mass in their wake as five desperate horsemen lashed their mounts for the sanctuary of the canyon maze, and killer Chav Cody even whispered a fervent prayer.

But no god worth his salt would heed the supplication of an outlaw on the run, and they was still a good half-mile from safety when trouble loomed from a shadowed crevice ahead and to their left.

Marshal Murdock had been hounding the gang for ten long days. He'd lost their trail up at Samson's Pass then reasoned that a veteran like Bannerman must make a try to reach Bright's County beyond the Sawteeth Divide – and the only navigable trail across this quarter of the mountains began down here at Twelve Canyons.

Murdock had figured dead right, yet it was a sense of bitter irony, not triumph, that dominated the gray manhunter's thinking as his big old sixgun began to roar. For in the long wait here in this godforsaken corner of the foothills he'd been powerless to prevent his town posse dwindling from an angry dozen to just one store clerk and two cowboys.

In contrast, Bannerman's bunch was six-strong, gunmen all, and riding for their very lives.

The brutally uneven clash that followed lasted no longer than a half-minute without slowing Bannerman's headlong progress by so much as a moment. The grim result was two possemen and one outlaw sprawled dead upon the bloody plain with nothing but a dwindling dust cloud to show the lawman where his murderous quarry had been swallowed up by the canyon maze.

Although as relentless a manhunter as Bleak County had ever known, Murdock made no attempt to give chase. An army could lose itself in that maze, and what was left of his strength was now down to virtually zero. All he could do was sit and nurse his wounds and wait in the hope of Bannerman losing himself in the network of canyons.

Some hope.

Bannerman, some said, boasted a relief map of the Dakotas for a nervous system.

Murdock showed no surprise when sunrise came and he held his battered old field glasses to his eyes, soon to detect the barely visible specks of riders ascending a goat track of a trail two thousand feet above, barely moving against the backdrop of the gray lava face of the Sawteeth which towered mightily above all like the ramparts of eternity.

The lawman spat tobacco juice and sleeved his mouth.

'Headin' fer Bright's,' he predicted. He was feeling low as whalebones, and they were at the bottom of the sea. But after a time the oldster brightened at a thought. The counties on either side of the Sawteeth were old enemies. Bleak County had always been dry and poor, Bright's lucky and rich. Now that smug Sheriff Bean, who treated him like a poor relation and never missed an opportunity to damage him in the eyes of the counties commissioner up in Monument, would shortly find himself playing host to as lethal a bunch of hellions as old hellion-hating Murdock had ever hunted.

Their 'loss', he realized, could well be Bleak County's gain.

He grinned for the first time in weeks and reached for the coffee. It was true what wise folks said, he mused sagely. Things rarely turn out as bad as you first fear.

Sometimes she would merely step lightly through the doors of the saloon, take a chair briefly just inside the batwings then be gone after but a few tantalizing minutes. But other times – the good times – she would come right on through to the mahogany bar where old Bo Fleet reigned over bottles and register in the best saloon in town, settle herself atop a felt-covered faro table and proceed to hold court for the young and the old, chatting, smiling, flirting or teasing, as pretty and impermanent as a May butterfly.

This had been her unusual habit for quite a time now, but because she was so pretty, cheeky and personable, her visits never grew commonplace. And even old Bo, sixty-four years old and weathered gray as a horned toad, would forget his cares, slick back what was left of his hair and just settle down to savor the moment whenever she showed.

'Best danged part of my whole week,' he was heard to observe at least once every day, 'is when that little lady shows up here Monday or Tuesday mornin's the way she does.'

She always came one day or the other, sometimes both. The early weekdays were usually quiet and relaxed at Chinnick's saloon – although ever since she'd begun stopping by it was surprising the number of towners found their way to Buffalo Horn's top watering-hole for a mid-morning pick-me-up, whereas they seemed quite capable of getting through the rest of the weekdays without such assistance.

Here, Buck Poley of Poley's Feed and Grain, and the telegraph operator, both men of middle years, rubbed shoulders with the young bucks and blades of the town around Buffalo Horn's main bar. The latter were there in force today, some content just to share her presence, others more intent on attracting the girl's attention, this despite the fact that she always managed to keep each man at arm's length while charming him silly, her very untouchableness a magnet they somehow just couldn't resist.

Her name was Della Honeysett, her father was wealthy Rory Honeysett, merchant, civic leader and president of the Honeysett Banking Company on Front Street. And she was just seventeen years old.

'Disgraceful carryings on!' many a respectable matron fulminated whenever the subject of Honeysett's youngest arose, conscious as they were that their very own menfolk might well be part of 'Della's court', finding those mornings at Chinnick's simply impossible to resist.

Of course her father objected strenuously to her behaviour – for all the good that did. Recently Honeysett had threatened to ship her off to Boston to a young ladies' finishing school if she didn't stop dragging the family name into disrepute. It was common knowledge that in response she'd threatened to jump a stage to the coast and ship out as a mess girl on a windjammer Orient-bound if he just tried.

Honeysett was no man to trifle with, but it seemed that while he boasted three other perfectly behaved and 'normal' daughters, his youngest handled him the same as she did her admirers at the saloon.

His response had been a threat to send one of his men along to Chinnick's to look out for his 'little girl' should her forward ways land her in trouble. It never went any further than that for her father knew what everyone in town had known for years – spirited, rebellious Della Honeysett could look out for herself, in any company.

'Knows how to look out for herself that lassie does,' old Bo liked to brag while pouring himself another and settling down to listen to her latest gossip about the parson and Mrs Austin from down by the tannery.

It was a Monday in early August a fortnight later when she showed; the first working day of a week that would never be forgotten in Buffalo Horn, although nobody had, as yet, any inkling of the cloud hovering over the prosperous town.

It was just another hot and still Dakota

morning with the saloon's green shades drawn against the glare shimmering up off Front. On hand were the regular loungers and barflies sipping their first cold beers, along with the dozen or so well-dressed men down along the bar sipping at their shots. Della's court was present in force today.

Today there were also two strangers present.

The first was a black-bearded fellow in filthy buckskins and a hat rimed with salt sweat, a wolf-hunter relaxing away from the solitude of the Sawteeth in town on his bi-annual blow-out.

The other was harder to classify. A powerfully built man of around thirty with rough-cut red hair and yellow-flecked eyes, he'd been hanging around town for several days not talking much, just drinking whiskey and meeting every curious glance with a glower that discouraged familiarity.

He called himself Reb and seemed to have made Chinnick's his base for however long he meant to stay. He had money for whiskey and asked a lot of questions, and even though he appeared something of a hardcase he hadn't caused any trouble thus far. This was wise. Strangers were neither plentiful nor particularly welcome in law-abiding Buffalo Horn, but were tolerated providing they kept the peace.

Burly Reb seemed ready to notch up another day of good behaviour – until Della Honeysett sashayed in.

As always she was dressed in showy yet stylish bright colors with flecks of salmon-colored lace showing at wrists and throat. She carried a fashionable summer straw hat and red leather pocket-book, which she removed and placed beside her when she perched atop the faro table while they brought her up to date on the latest gossip. She then leaned back, swinging one long silken leg and tossing her curls as young Jim Easy related details of the sad weekend mishap of Ace Smith. Seemed Ace had been locked out by his lady wife Saturday. His attempt to gain ingress to his backstreet castle through the attic window with the help of a stepladder resulted in a fifteen-foot drop and a busted leg.

Everybody chuckled at the story, and the girl's lilting laughter seemed to reach every male ear in the room. But while most responded with a smile or nod, it was the man who called himself Reb who seemed most affected, so much so that he set his glass aside and started deliberately across the room towards the group like a seafarer heeding the siren's song.

Nobody noticed. Old Bo was setting up another round, chuckled when Della teasingly asked young Easy if it had been him hanging around her bedroom window late last night – just to see him blush.

'Ah, missy, is it any wonder our eyes get all bloodshot just strainin' for a glimpse of you any Monday,' Old Bo chuckled. He set a glass of lemonade down on the bar just in case she might drink it and was meticulously wiping down the bar when he looked up to see the big stranger homing in on her circle of admirers.

His smile vanished. If a man didn't develop a sure nose for trouble after forty years behind a bar he was in the wrong business. There was something about the man he didn't care for, something unsettling in the way he walked and the glitter in his eyes.

The stranger shoved Buck Poley aside and stood with legs astride before Della.

'Hey there, Blue-eyes,' he said in a whiskey-roughened voice. 'The name's Reb.'

An abrupt silence engulfed the group and hostile eyes cut to the intruder. But the man seemed unaware. He only had eyes for this girl. In response, Della returned his gaze coolly.

'First name Johnny?' she quipped.

The stranger slapped his thigh and roared with mirth.

'Johnny Reb? Dang bust me but you're a right cheeky little filly, Blue-eyes ... figgered that the second you showed. And let me tell you if ever a bunch of stuffed shirts and namby-pamby dudes needed brightenin' up it's these momma's boys.' He winked broadly and swayed just a little. He was drinking doubles. 'So how's about I buy you a shot and give you the chance to get acquainted with a real man, huh?'

'Now see here–' began young Jim Easy indignantly, but Della, slipping gracefully from the table and taking up hat and pocketbook, spoke over him.

'I was just leaving, Jim.' The narrow-eyed glance she gave the young man and the others was a warning to keep calm. 'I've arranged to meet my sisters at Bilby's store.' She nodded politely to the hard-faced stranger. 'Pleased to have met you, Mr Reb.'

Everybody relaxed. It was plain the big man was out for trouble. But Della had sensed it too, and dealt with it as only she could.

They thought.

But as the group were making reluctant farewells, and Della Honeysett blew a kiss to a relieved-looking old Bo, big Reb's rough voice made itself heard again.

'Now there's no call to be gettin' skittish

with me, girl. I don't mean no harm. Just bein' sociable is all.' He paused, his grin forced, then added softly, 'Back where I hail from it's seen as kinda bad manners for a lady to refuse a gentleman's invitation ... if you get what I mean?'

The silence that followed had a pulsing quality to it, as the saloon realized two things simultaneously: this man was drunker than they'd realized. He also looked dangerous.

'I do appreciate your offer, sir, but I don't drink and I really do have an appointment.'

Reb's rat-trap smile vanished. 'Now don't hand me that malarkey, Blue-eyes. I know a sport when I see one. I was watchin' you from over yonder, settin' up on the table and showin' your legs and–'

'That'll be enough, mister,' interjected the telegrapher. 'Whoever you might be, you don't have the right to speak to Miss Honeysett that way. She's a lady.'

'Please, Gus,' Della began, but already the stranger was rounding on the telegrapher, eyes narrowed to yellow slits.

'Go fry, bucko!' he said in a voice that cut. He made a slashing gesture with a powerful arm. 'All of you go fry. You reckon I ain't been sizin' up all you popinjays and nancy-boys and soft-fingered lick-spittles the last few days?' His lip curled in contempt. 'Dancin' round this filly like a bunch of geldings – like you know there's somethin' you want only you can't remember what it is. Well, I ain't no geldin'. I'm buyin' her a drink and any son of a bitch who don't like it had better be ready to toe-dance on account he's gonna have lead hornets buzzin' round his boots right smart!'

In case they didn't get the notion, the redhead slapped the worn wooden handle of the .44 sagging from a battered holster tied low round the thigh. The whole room was still. For the man called Reb had called it as it was. These were all good solid citizens. But they weren't barroom brawlers and scarce any of them even wore a sixgun, whereas the man prowling up and down before them with that sneer on his face looked like he might have been sporting that ugly old cutter since grade school.

To their shame, no man spoke.

The only person in the whole place who showed no sign of fear suddenly strode purposefully towards the batwings with a staccato click of high heels.

Instantly Reb grabbed out his gun, face darkening angrily.

'Just you hold it right there, Blue-eyes!'

She stopped, poised and unafraid. 'I take back what I said to you, mister.'

'Yeah? Well, that's more like it.'

'I said it was nice to meet you, but it isn't,' she flashed back. 'Now I really am leaving. And you can put that stupid gun away. You have no idea how ridiculous you look.'

With that she turned away, walking neither swiftly nor slowly towards the doors. The stranger's face mirrored a moment's confusion which was quickly replaced by a look of brutish wrath. Without a word he raised the weapon, training it on the slim, blue-ginghamed back and deliberately thumbed back the hammer.

It was Jack Taylock who correctly read his murderous purpose, and reacted accordingly.

'Della!' he shouted desperately. 'Stop!'

Something of the fear in the man's voice touched the girl and halted her, still some twenty feet short of the swinging doors. She turned smoothly, composed still, but pale now. From the bar, Reb stared at her over his gunsights. Slowly his face wreathed with a wolfish grin. He lowered his weapon to waist-level, but it was still trained on her breasts.

'Plague it, sister,' he panted, sounding actually relieved. 'You damn near made me bore you.'

'Do you always shoot women in the back, Mr Johnny Reb?'

Reb wasn't fazed. 'Cain't really recall the last time I had to do that. Most gals don't force me to. Some gals even reckon old Reb's a barrel of fun. Could be you will too if you give me half a chance. Now come on back to this li'l ol' bar and be neighbourly.'

She shook her head deliberately. 'I don't

know who you are or where you hail from, but I do know you can't go around threatening people with guns in Buffalo Horn. We have a sheriff here – and a jail.'

The man brushed a hand across his eyes and for a moment appeared almost uncertain in the face of her cool contempt. But when he replied he sounded strong enough.

'I said come back here, Blue-eyes!'

This time Della made no reply. There was only the faintest lifting of a finely sculpted chin, a challenging flash of long-lashed eyes. But to the regulars of Chinnick's these little mannerisms were clear indications that Honeysett's daughter was in defiant mode. And there was no record of her ever having backed down once she'd made a stand.

It was a stand-off and it was time for someone to come to her aid – before her spirit and stubbornness got this girl killed.

Yet still no man moved. Neither Buck Poley or Gus McCoy, nor young Jack Taylock or Jim Easy, the boy who dreamed of someday making Rory Honeysett's daughter his bride. Instead, they all just stood, only half-believing what they were seeing – the look in the man's eyes, the big gun in his paw, the air of menace coming off the fellow like heat off a furnace.

Big Reb Houston, for that was the stranger's full name, sweated inside his buckskin jacket and prayed the damned jade would just turn and come back to him, otherwise he might well be forced to keep his word and shoot. He'd gone too far but didn't know how to back out of it. She'd either do as he said, or he wouldn't be able to lower his weapon unfired.

In that electric moment the batwings opened inwards and a man walked in. Automatically every eye searched him out, watching him as he halted with the sun-glare in back of him, adjusting his eyes to the cool gloom of the shuttered room.

There was something about him standing there, something both commanding and challenging that was enough to divert their attention despite the harrowing atmosphere holding the big room in its grip.

He was little over average height, lithe and youthfully muscled. His face was dark brown from the sun, young and fine-boned. His mouth was full with a habitual quirk to one corner, as though he constantly found amusement in the world around him. But the eyes were old and of a strange cold blue that gave the lie to the twist of the mouth. He wore tight-fitting rig with a dusty hat thrust back from black curls and carried a single handgun thonged down on the right thigh. He was a stranger in Buffalo Horn.

It was a full ten seconds before the newcomer casually strolled across to where Della Honeysett stood. His walk was half-stealth, half-swagger. He stood at the girl's side but stared directly at Houston.

'Shootin' before lunch?' he said with a hint of humor. His voice was as distinctive as his appearance, soft yet steely, not much more than a loud whisper, yet it carried.

To general astonishment, the menacing Reb had turned pale at the stranger's entry.

His whiskey flush was replaced by a film of fine sweat. Reb had slipped from menace to acute discomfort in mere moments. Instead of replying he chose to stare down at the gun in his hand.

The stranger left Della's side and crossed to the bar. Leaning an elbow on the polished surface, he allowed his eyes to play slowly and almost insolently over the assembled towners before returning his attention to Houston.

'You're drunk!' The whispery voice had a lash to it.

Twin spots of anger suffused Houston's cheeks.

'Goddamnit, I–'

'Stinkin' drunk. You haven't shaved this mornin', you stink like a skunk carcass and you're actin' like you left your brains someplace else.'

'I don't have to take this.'

'You're still pointin' that cutter my way, Reb,' the stranger said. 'Put it away.'

'The hell I will!'

'Put it up, I said!'

Nobody seemed to breathe as they watched the troublemaker gripped with indecision, gun still in hand, feet spread wide and head thrust forward like a tormented animal. The slim young man with the cold eyes didn't move, yet somehow looked terribly dangerous: relaxed and dangerous. They fully expected Reb to rebel, yet after a dragging quarter-minute he stifled a curse and thrust the weapon back into its holster. He glared belligerently at the newcomer.

'All right – hotshot,' he hissed. 'I done what you said. And now I'm gettin' to hell out of this crummy dump.' He paused, and when he continued his voice was heavy with sarcasm. 'That's if it's all right with you, of course.'

The young man was looking bored. 'Matter of fact it's not, Reb.'

Houston appeared to be in danger of choking. Someone sniggered. His eyes were red.

'Damn your eyes, Shannon–'

'Button up.' For the first time the young

man turned his eyes to look directly at Della. 'You were treatin' this girl a mite roughly when I happened by. Best you apologize before you leave.'

Della said quickly, 'I'm sure you've done enough, sir.' Her voice seemed to hold a suppressed excitement as their eyes met. 'I don't hold a grudge.'

A slow smile crossed the young man's face, revealing strong white teeth.

'Mebbe you don't, miss, but I sure do.' He turned to Houston and the smile vanished as quickly as it had appeared. 'I'm waitin', Reb.'

'I'll see you in hell first.'

To the onlookers, it seemed that the new-comer shrugged unconcernedly as though suddenly uninterested in the situation now. But quicker than the eye could follow he spun and threw a lightning punch from the shoulder. Houston shook to the bootheels with the impact of the vicious blow, his jaws snapping open with pain and shock. A whistling uppercut closed his mouth with a snap like a rat-trap, sending him reeling down the length of the bar to collapse to the floor.

Shadow-swift, the other followed to yank him to his feet in one effortless motion. Keeping his voice low so that only Houston could hear, he hissed,

'Apologize, Reb, or I'll kill you. I mean it.'

Houston, bloody-mouthed and half-conscious, stared into the chilling eyes so close to his own and seemed to read his own death there in their blue depths. All bravado and bluster left him in a rush, leaving the hard man trembling.

'All right, all right,' he groaned, trying to find the girl through blurring eyes. 'I'm sorry, Blue – er, Miss.'

'I accept, Mr Reb.'

Houston turned uncertainly to his tormentor, who was handing him his hat. Blue eyes mocked him now.

'Don't come back, Reb,' he whispered. Then contemptuously he walked past, going to the girl's side, offering bloody-mouthed

Houston the width of his muscular back.

Something came alive in Houston's eyes, some last spark of rebellion, but was quickly gone. With a last muttered curse he lurched past the couple and went out through the swinging doors.

Immediately the voices bubbled up, relieved voices, astonished voices, curious voices. Who was the stranger? How come he knew the troublemaker? Was his name Shannon, or had they heard Reb wrong? And the question nobody was asking quite yet; how come Della was studying this stranger as though he'd come wrapped in cloth of gold and with a halo round his head?

Anxious to re-establish himself in the girl's eyes, Jim Easy strode across to the couple. He cleared his throat and both glanced his way.

'Come have a drink, Della,' he said, wondering just how scared he must have appeared during the drama. 'There'll never be a better reason, I reckon. And you too, of course, mister,' he added, giving the young stranger a man-to-man look and extending his hand. 'I've never seen anything braver than what you just did.'

He let his hand drop, face flushing when the other showed no inclination to take it. And Della said quietly:

'I don't care for a drink, Jim.'

'Me neither,' affirmed the whispering voice.

By this time all the drinkers were grouped around the pair, and Taylock said curiously:

'Er, that man called you Shannon, was it?'

'That's right.'

'That your first or second name?' someone asked.

'Just Shannon.'

'We're all beholden to you son,' said Old Bo.

'Yeah?' Shannon's tone was cold. 'You shouldn't have to be. Seems to me there was more than enough of you to handle a bum like Reb Houston. What sort of town is this anyway?'

Heads hung. They stood accused. And in

the silence, displaying the same insolence towards them that he'd shown the trouble-maker, Shannon turned his back on them all, and said:

'See you home – Della, is it?'

No 'miss', no fawning flattery, yet Della's reaction was something every male present would have given his last dollar to elicit. With a smile none had ever seen before, she smiled acceptance, even flushing slightly which caused her to look even lovelier than ever. She appeared entranced by this stranger, and if one could see past the arrogant poise of the man, it seemed he was equally impressed in turn.

This was impossible, of course. But how could they doubt the testimony of their own eyes as the friends of five minutes made their way to the doors of Chinnick's saloon, seemingly oblivious of everything but one another.

Jack Taylock, who like his friend Jim Easy, had a powerful and not-so-secret ambition to one day become far more than just an amusing companion to wealthy Rory Honey-sett's headstrong youngest daughter, said peevishly:

'Heck, it's okay to be grateful – but I think Della's overdoing it some. Why, she's practically simpering at that fellow.'

'Feller's got something though, ain't he, boy?' grinned old Bo Fleet, not helping at all.

'Looks like a gunslinger if you ask me,' weighed in an equally disgruntled Jim Easy as they flowed out onto the gallery. 'And he knows that no-account Reb, remember? Wouldn't surprise me any if he's on the dodge.'

'Goddamn!' Taylock exclaimed. 'Look what she's doing now!'

They could see only too well. Della had taken the man's arm, and his head was inclined towards hers as they approached a mean-eyed roan gelding standing at the hitch rail, rolling its eyes. Passers by halted to stare when the young woman boldly slipped her arm through the stranger's, and a voice suspiciously like that of town gossip,

34

Hetty Peel, was heard to gasp; 'Land sakes, what is that child up to now?'

As though in response to the query, Shannon untied his horse and swung up. Watchers gasped when he kicked his boot clear of the stirrup, leaned from the saddle and hauled the girl up behind him.

Chinnick's gallery and the central block itself seemed beyond comment as they watched Della Honeysett link her arms around the stranger's slim waist as they swung away down Front Street, her stylish bonnet jiggling in rhythm to the horse's gait.

Even Hetty Peel seemed too shocked for speech now. Not even a saloon girl would dream of riding double. And astride to boot!

As several drinkers moved out into the sunlight to watch the double-laden horse recede, Buck Poley said hoarsely:

'If old Rory looks out his office window and sees his daughter riding off with–'

'He's just taking her home, is all,' Jim Easy predicted, fanning himself with his hat. 'Could be she's too shook up to walk.'

But the two on the big roan horse didn't swing in at the imposing Honeysett house. They rode right on by, seemingly oblivious of the sea of astonished faces they were leaving behind. When last sighted, swinging round the corner into Austin Street which led to the trail out of town, they were laughing.

There was silence for a full moment after they vanished from sight. Then Old Bo Fleet, looking suddenly gray around the gills, turned to his companions and said:

'Somebody better go tell her father.'

CHAPTER 2

POSSE

'Mr Honeysett.'

'Yes, madam?'

'Sir, something important has arisen and I feel you should know–' 'Madam' cut in the short stocky president of the Honeysett Banking Company with ill-concealed impatience, 'if this something important has no relationship to the immediate concerns of my guest and the Tocsin Hills Mining Company, I suggest you absent yourself this instant – if you value your position.'

The middle-aged woman standing in the doorway paled. She was Honeysett's personal secretary and general factotum. Better than most she knew how difficult her boss could be, yet such were her concerns at the moment that she somehow found the courage to stand her ground. 'Please, Mr Honeysett, it's about your–'

'Thank you, madam!'

That did it. The door hissed closed and Honeysett pressed thumb and forefinger to the corners of his eyes.

'Damn and double damn!' he muttered, which was mild for a volcanic son of old Ireland who could go off like a dynamite charge when the spirit moved him. He blinked at the man seated across his huge mahogany desk. 'Now, where were we, Jacob?'

'Security, Mr Honeysett,' replied the balding mining representative. 'Of course, of course, security.' Honeysett spread pudgy hands with an engaging smile. 'What else could it be, eh, my friend?'

Most days around this time in the summer the banker would quit his office on the second floor above his fine brick bank building and head across Front Street to the Cattlemen's Club for a few light refreshers followed by lunch and the amiable company of fellow businessmen, cattlemen, miners and others of the moneyed élite of Bright's County.

Today was different.

He'd been sequestered in his private office since nine with strict instructions against being interrupted, while he conclaved with a representative of the Tocsin Hills Mining Company. The man had come to town specifically to finalize arrangements for one of the most responsible undertakings the bank had ever been called upon to handle. Namely, the depositing over the coming weekend of a huge gold shipment from the mine, an estimated 100,000 dollars' worth.

Up until now, Honeysett had been fully involved in the conference, but the interruption – plus his growing thirst – was affecting his concentration.

He stole a glance from his big picture-window at the false-fronts opposite. Thin dust, the eternal summer dust of Buffalo Horn, wafted up mistily past the window-glass, rising from hoofs and wheels on the main stem. He could almost taste the splendid Scotch whiskey the club stocked especially for their most powerful member.

Whiskey had played a large part in Honeysett's life. His father in old Ireland had drunk himself to death on the stuff leaving young Rory no option but to head for the New World, where he first worked for, then owned and eventually expanded hugely, a whiskey-importing company.

The whiskey business led him into banking

where a combination of avarice and natural business acumen quickly saw him set up in the West with his own bank, a dozen thriving enterprises, fine house, wonderful family and prospects everywhere he looked.

Sometime he felt he had it all, but right now all he really wanted was a stiff drink.

He blinked upon realizing his guest was now discussing his vault and his concerns regarding it.

'I've told you, Jack, that vault can not be opened by a single soul but myself,' Honeysett insisted.

'Combination locks have been cracked before.'

'If somebody has the combination, I agree.' Honeysett tapped his temple. 'But the combination's known only to me and it's not written anyplace. It's all in here.'

Although his visitor seemed satisfied with this, he continued to drone on boringly, and Honeysett continued to grapple with his thirst until he slowly grew aware of the sound of rising voices from the outer office, this despite his strict instructions against any sort of distraction.

At last, an excuse for winding up this Tocsin gasbag, he thought. 'Pardon me, Sam,' he said, jumping to his feet. He was out through the door in a shot to deal with the minions.

He propped on confronting a crowd comprising a full half of his staff supplemented by a number of towners amongst whom he spotted his daughters, old Bo from Chinnick's and craggy-faced Sheriff Bean.

'What in the name of St Patrick–' he began, but his assistant interrupted.

'I tried to tell you, Mr Honeysett–'

'Tell me what?' he barked, cleaving his way through to the lawman. 'What the devil's going on, man?'

The lawman swallowed twice, then blurted it out.

'It ... it's your youngest, Mr Honeysett. She's ... she's...'

'In the name of mortal sin – what, man?'

His eldest daughter, Milly, appeared at his

side. Her pretty face was ashen.

'Della's gone off with a stranger. Run away perhaps. Oh, Papa, what are we going to do?'

Honeysett sagged. Oh for a double. Perhaps a treble. As a man of the world he knew female progeny could be difficult, but his youngest could turn simple difficulty into a science.

'All right,' he sighed, dropping into a padded chair. 'Give me the details. And, Janet, fetch me a drink!'

Within minutes he'd heard it all and was back on his feet, once again the man of decisive action and authority the town knew so well. His instructions were emphatic and non-negotiable. A posse was to be formed to follow the trail his daughter and the stranger had taken, and he would head it up personally. In addition, smaller parties of searchers were to comb the minor trails and report back to the jailhouse if anything was discovered.

That done, he sent his weeping daughters home to their grandmother, ordered his staff back to work, then strode for the stairs with the sheriff and his deputy trotting behind him like flunkies, which in a very real sense they were.

Hitting Front, he was gratified to see a dozen or more men, most of them young clients of Chinnick's, waiting for him. Jim Easy, Jack Taylock and other would-be suitors of his youngest announced they were ready to ride with him just as far as it took, and the tough Irishman in him responded to the fact that most were armed.

But being Rory Honeysett, a glaringly obvious question sprang to mind as he drew on his gloves and prepared to mount his beautiful saddle horse:

'If this story I'm told of what occurred is so, how come you brave buckos didn't stop this spalpeen abducting my little girl?'

To a man they looked uncomfortable. They had every reason to keep silent. But Bo Fleet was an old man who told it like it was.

'Begging your pardon, Rory, but from where I was standing it was a question of who was abducting who.'

The banker let that sink in. His jaw muscles worked. He was a kind and loving parent but also something of a domestic tyrant. At home, everyone did as he said. Everyone but his youngest, that was.

His eyes glittered dangerously as he swung a leg over his horse's back and settled into the saddle before a hundred onlookers.

After this, that finishing school in the East for Mistress Della was no longer a possibility, but a probability.

'Ho!' he hollered at the top of his lungs, and led the fifty-man posse out for the west trail.

The tracks of the roan horse proved easy to follow until they reached the limestone belt five miles from town. Here, not even a fully laden Conestoga with metal rimmed wheels would leave any sign, much less a horse with two slender riders.

Even so they split up into search parties, scouring the terrain in ever-widening circles as a pitiless sun raged down. It was too hot even to curse.

They found nothing.

There were expert trackers in the party but none was unable to come up with a single clue as to which direction Shannon's mean-eyed roan had been taken.

Soon the soft-handed clerks and pale-faced saloon lizards amongst the party were glancing ruefully back towards the town, and eventually the sheriff called a halt to the search in order to discuss the situation further.

Honeysett immediately took over the discussion and wouldn't let go of it.

The tycoon wouldn't hear of disbanding. Instead he formed the searchers up into squads of four and sent them back towards town to scour both sides of the trail in case they'd misread the sign and Shannon might have quit the trail and taken another direction.

It was a forlorn hope and it was Honeysett himself who finally called a halt to the search while the sun was still an hour from the horizon. There were no tracks, there would be none. This was all too plain by now. They'd be better off heading back in the slender hope that they mind find some positive news awaiting them there.

Some hope.

Nightfall found Honeysett slumped at the head of the huge dining-table he'd had shipped out to the Dakotas at great expense all the way from New York City, all alone but for his bottle and his thoughts.

He'd given his womenfolk an hour's weeping and wailing then sent them packing. He was all worried out, so moodily switched his thoughts instead to business, an old habit in troubled times that never ceased to work for him.

It worked now as he reviewed the visit by the boss of Tocsin Hills mine just ten days earlier. The bank had successfully handled large amounts of gold for Tocsin before and Honeysett was expecting a similar assignment on this occasion, something around the $20,000 mark. Instead he discovered the mine had been stockpiling over recent months and the value of freight they planned to ship to Doolinville via Buffalo Horn was closer to $100,000.

The gold would be brought from the mines to Buffalo Horn next Friday under heavy guard, lodged at the bank over the weekend then taken on for its destination under a heavy military escort from Fort Small the following Monday.

It was a challenge, of course. But pugnacious Honeysett had thrived on such all his life, and was ready to bet all he owned that he would oversee the huge operation through to a successful conclusion, just like always.

He splashed whiskey as sweet as honey and golden as a Kerry sunrise into his glass and took a powerful swig, big heavy creases furrowing his brow now. If only he was as successful at fatherhood as at business!

He sighed heavily as traditional Irish melancholy stole over him. Of course, the paradox was that his most troublesome daughter was his favorite and always had been. Milly, Cassie and Shirleen were wonderful, dutiful and loving young women while Della had been difficult, challenging, loving and a constant threat to his peace of mind almost from the cradle.

Even so, he was still stunned to think that Della, who was somehow able to manipulate, intrigue, con and simply dazzle jut about every male he'd ever seen cross her sights since girlhood, would have simply ridden away with a wild-looking cowboy on an ugly big horse without a thought for the consequences. Even by her questionable standards that was going a tad far.

He was feeling sorry for himself again, and was reaching for the whiskey when he became aware of the commotion from somewhere outside.

He blinked owlishly. Last time today he'd heard voices outside his door, bad news had been the culprit. Could this mean more of the same?

The hell if it did!

He poured another and had the goblet

half-way to his lips when his Mexican body-servant came rushing into the room unannounced waving his arms excitedly and yelling; '*Señor, señor!* Outside now. You must see. *Ven cuanto antes!*'

The man vanished in an instant leaving Buffalo Horn's most powerful and peeved citizen to trudge out after him, following his dancing figure out across the balcony to the front lawns where a crowd was rapidly gathering as a double-laden horse slowly approached the big heavy *zaguán* gates which kept the lower classes from encroaching upon the meticulously kept Honeysett turf.

He barely saw the people or even his womenfolk lined up at the gates. He was staring with his jaw hanging open as the cowboy astride the big ugly roan gelding brought his mount to a halt.

Behind the cowboy sat Della!

The banker's first reaction was strange. Instead of rushing to his daughter's side as she swung to the ground as lightly as a

49

feather, he twisted his neck to stare upwards at his mother's window. Sure enough, there she was in the lamplight, hands on hips and smiling smugly down at him with that infuriating I-told-you-so look stamped upon her lined old face.

Of all the people who'd proffered their own notion on just what might have befallen his daughter, only his difficult little old Irish mother, Clara Honeysett – whom his youngest offspring most closely resembled as everyone agreed – insisted that Della had simply gone off innocently horse-backing with a young man and would return home in her own good time.

He cursed. He jerked round at that sound of a voice.

'Have you been drinking, papa?'

He stared at his daughter. She looked exactly as she had when he'd last seen her that morning, fresh-faced and perfectly groomed in that flamboyant way she had, swinging her hat on her finger and daring to show just a small frown of disapproval as she glanced at the bottle which he hadn't realized he'd carried out with him.

It seemed a long time before he let a held breath escape.

'Is that all you have to say to me, young lady?'

'Well, no. What's all the fuss about? Why are the girls crying and carrying on?'

'Why...?' he half-choked, then broke off. That mean-looking horse had hung its head over his expensive gate and the young rider, seated so nonchalantly in the saddle, seemed to be studying him with an expression of ill-concealed contempt.

Honeysett took several steps forward, halted. He studied the fine-boned face with the strange blue eyes, instinctively sensing the man's controlled power and a vitality that hid itself in apparent indolence.

'You the man they call Shannon?'

The rider nodded but didn't speak. The girls' maid had just burst from the house to embrace Della. The three elder sisters joined in the celebration. Honeysett's head began to ache as Sheriff Bean came through the side-gate and approached.

'Congratulations, Mr Honeysett.' The man jerked a thumb over his shoulder. 'Er ... do you want this man arrested?'

'You're damned right I do–'

'Oh, Papa, don't be absurd.' Della detached herself from the others and strolled past the two men towards the gate before halting. 'We went riding, is all,' she said, turning. 'I can't believe that's a crime even by your standards, Sheriff Bean.'

'How dare you!' the banker yelled, finally losing his temper. 'The least you could do is show a little concern, madam. The whole town's been upset, not to mention how I felt, and the girls. I never expected much of you, Della, but...'

'No, you haven't expected much of me, Papa. Except to be some sort of mechanical toy doll who cries and says mama when you wind the goddamn thing up...'

'Della!' Milly cried, shocked. 'Please don't curse before everyone.'

'Oh hush, sis. I went riding with a young man and you'd think it was Fort Sumter all over again.' Standing with hands on hips and suddenly smiling, she glanced up at the man on the roan who lifted a lazy eyebrow in acknowledgement.

'We followed your tracks,' the banker said sternly, barely maintaining control. 'You quit the trail at the limestone slopes and we couldn't pick it up again. Where did you go?'

People were hanging over the fence to listen. This was the most excitement respectable Buffalo Horn had seen in some time.

'Why, cross-country to Sylvan Springs where we always go on picnics, of course,' came the bland response. 'And we had one. Jerked meat and a bottle of mescal. That's what I call a picnic.'

Honeysett heard the girls' shocked murmurings and the angry voices of the men, some of whom had ridden with him throughout the long afternoon.

He felt suddenly old, tired and very angry. Della had caused him embarrassment many a time but never so seriously or publicly. Certainly he'd feared for her safety, he defended himself. But now she was back safe he was solely concerned about Rory Honeysett. Most difficulties in life for this man stemmed from the simple fact that, beneath his veneer as father, citizen and caring patriarch of this town, he was truly only concerned about himself.

His bleak stare cut back to the cause of it all, the laconic horseman who through the whole incident had not spoken a word. A saddle bum! He'd encountered the breed often enough in the past, yet they were mercifully rare about Bright's County. A troublemaker, almost certainly, but luckily alone.

It was at such times that his powerful position offered great advantages. In time of crisis his word was virtually law. Virtually every responsible citizen in Buffalo Horn from the lamplighter up to Sheriff Bean stood square behind him in times of trouble. They couldn't afford not to.

'What's your name, mister?' he demanded.

'You know it.' The husky whisper, eyes as unfathomable as great distance.

'Shannon isn't a complete name.'

'You don't like it?'

Honeysett felt himself reddening. 'You don't seem to get the idea, mister. You're a total stranger in Buffalo Horn, and we expect strangers to give an account of themselves. You've caused a great deal of trouble today, which could land you in a serious bind. So, now that you understand me, I'll ask again. What is your name?'

'You're Irish, aren't you?'

'And what the devil has that to do with anything?'

'They named a river after me over there. Shannon.'

One man was stupid enough to laugh out loud. There were suppressed sniggers. But most were scowling at the rider now. He'd thrown the whole town into upheaval today and everyone saw him as the cause of it all. Della, of course, was blameless – as usual. The sheriff spoke drily.

'I just might have to show you the inside of a cell if you don't do better than that, son.'

'You will do no such thing, Wal Bean,' Della said fiercely. 'This idiocy has gone far enough. We went riding together, Mr Shannon showed himself to be a fine gentleman, and now we're back home. What on earth more is there to be said?'

'Silence!' Honeysett thundered. 'Girls, mama, escort Miss Della into the house. This is man's business from here on in.'

Mama Chondo, a burly, brown-skinned woman who'd bullied and spoiled the girls since birth, put her hand lightly on Della's arm and murmured something, but the girl shook her off angrily.

'It's all too stupid,' she cried. 'It's too stupid for words.'

'Best do as he says, Della.'

It was Shannon who spoke, his entire manner altering when he addressed the girl. Everyone noted this change, but there was something stranger still. Della's reaction.

'All right, Shannon,' she said sweetly,

smiling in dimpling submission. 'If you say so.' She turned for the house but paused for a parting shot. 'Don't do anything foolish, Papa. There's no reason to.'

She swept the assembled crowd with the same warning look before disappearing with the women. The moment she was gone, unfriendly attention focused on the man on the roan horse. His offensive familiarity with Della, and her response to it, laid bare a raw streak of jealousy in virtually every man present. Men on horseback moved in closer round the roan, joining with those afoot to form a menacing semi-circle by the gates.

But the young rider just sat there looking lazy, although there was nothing casual in the way he spoke.

'I like your daughter, Honeysett. There's no call to get into a ringtail about that.'

'Boy, this here's a good town, a law-abiding town. We take pride in that – and we look after our own. You wander in out of no place at all, get involved in a saloon brawl, then disappear with my daughter causing no end of concern and touching off a manhunt involving half a hundred people.'

Honeysett paused for effect. He enjoyed playing the role of injured father and outraged citizen.

'So, if you don't come up with a bucketful of sensible answers, such as who you are and what you are doing here, Sheriff Bean might well have to lock you up until you change your mind.'

Shannon smiled mockingly.

'A good town you say, banker? A town where just being a stranger is a crime, and where the law takes its orders from fat businessmen? That's your notion of good?'

'Now see here–' Bean began heatedly, but Honeysett cut him off.

'I'm not going to argue with you, drifter–'

'Well, I'm arguing with you.' The strange voice had assumed sudden authority. 'You accuse me of ridin' in and startin' somethin'. Mister, when I got to Chinnick's a saddle tramp was fixin' to shoot your daughter in the back while most of these outraged citizens of yours here were just standin' there waitin' to see him do it. I stopped somethin' that was far worse than any fight – not started it. Did these heroes tell you that?'

Honeysett seemed to deflate visibly. He had not heard that version of events at the saloon. 'An unpleasant incident', was how Easy had described it. A sideways glance at the towners told him he'd most likely just heard the real truth. Finally.

'And as far as your daughter is concerned,' Shannon continued, 'I figured she was pretty upset and it'd be best to get her away from town for a while. Turned out she was upset – real upset. Know why? It wasn't so much the bum but the fact that folks she'd always figured as gentlemen and friends turned out to be nothin' better than a pack of cowards who wouldn't lift a finger to save her from a drunk with a gun.'

Whether an angry Jim Easy actually meant to reach for his sixgun, or if his sudden gesture was accidental, was unclear. But there was no misunderstanding the reaction.

Shannon's right shoulder dipped and a big Navy Colt appeared in his fist, trained squarely on Easy's shirt front.

It was a long taut time before they realized he wasn't about to shoot, allowing an ashen Easy to merge backwards into the throng, sleeving sweat off his face. Then as the stand-off eased some, Shannon lowered his gun barrel and the banker read the gesture as a cue to start in talking again – until he realized nobody was listening.

Buffalo Horn had put in a hard day. There'd been violence, upheaval and drama climaxing in this showdown where the mob had been ready to vent their spleen on the stranger until the sudden flash of a sixgun exposed their want of backbone yet again.

The mob had been playing a risky game; now they realized that a man like this man was far more adept at such games than they. It was a valuable lesson to learn without the spilling of blood.

Then abruptly that menacing gun was back in leather and the young rider swung his horse away from the *zaguán* gates with an avenue opening up in the mob before him.

He moved off without a backward glance, allowing the cayuse to pick its own leisurely pace as they slowly receded along darkening Front Street.

Immediately the mob began to break up. They quit the scene in ones and twos, some mumbling meaningless apologies to Bean and Honeysett, all anxious to be gone now, to go lick their wounds and salve their pride. Until at last just two men stood alone by the sheriff's prad, gazing back at the reassuring lights of the big house.

'Rory...' Bean began uncomfortably.

'Not now, man,' Honeysett said with a dismissive gesture. 'It's been a long day.'

He turned and made his way up the flagged pathway toward the lights as the hoofbeats of the lawman's horse faded.

'Too damn long, by God and by glory!' he panted. But tomorrow would be different. He would shape it his way. He always did.

CHAPTER 3

CAME THE JACKALS

The leather-topped brougham cleared the grove of Jeffrey pines to afford the travellers from the East their first glimpse of Buffalo Horn and the Sawteeth Range to the west. It had been a testing journey for Nate Wylder and his party and first glimpse of their destination seemed less than rewarding.

At least so thought big Matt Hancock. In his time in Wylder's employ he had visited many Dakota towns and regarded himself as something of an expert. He grudgingly supposed Buffalo Horn looked prosperous enough with its clean wide streets and large buildings, but it sure didn't look too exciting.

Leaning forward from the rear seat he

occupied with Stack, Hancock peered over Wylder's shoulder and said, 'Not too late to change your mind about this burg, boss.'

'Why – don't tell me you can't smell it already, big feller,' grinned Wylder, plying the ribbons with the skill that marked most everything he did.

'Smell the hayseed, you mean?'

'Don't crack wise, mister. Opportunity, is what I'm talking about. Sweetest scent this side of heaven.'

The big man sighed and leaned back against his cushioned leather seat as a smiling Wylder took a cigar from the breast pocket of his tailored English hunting-jacket and took his first close-up look at Buffalo Horn in over a year.

An impressive man in his prime with thick black hair and con man's winning smile, Wylder travelled far and wide in search for the next easy mark, the big hit – even the little old granny living alone in a shotgun cabin with a mangy dog her only company and $50,000 gathering mildew in the local bank might not be overlooked whenever he came to town.

He grinned around his cigar and livened the horses up with a slap of the reins. He never felt better than during the early stages of an operation when expectations ran strong and excitement was high. When he'd spent a week glad-handing and living it up in Rory Honeysett's town a year ago, midway through an exploratory sweep of Bright's County searching for 'opportunities', he'd made friends with everyone who counted here while assessing the place's potential as a target for the sting or a big hit. On that occasion, he'd decided Buffalo Horn was certainly prosperous enough, yet without boasting anything really tempting or sizable enough to attract the professional attentions of a big-time operator like himself.

On checking out of the Federation Hotel that last day, he'd a strong hunch he wouldn't have reason to stroll down Front Street again.

So much for hunches.

Just one year later he found himself back again. Salivating. And felt moved right now to congratulate himself on the foresight of his policy of continually spreading himself far and wide across his Dakotas stamping grounds, making contacts by the hundreds, never knowing which one of these might pay off someday, big time.

Before him lay a solid Midwestern commercial center, but in Wylder's imagination it more resembled a golden goose ripe for the plucking.

Through his many contacts and affiliations backed up by the plain old-fashioned buying of information, the man now skilfully guiding the sturdy four-wheeled brougham down off the slopes towards the town bridge, was now aware that this coming weekend, the bank of his 'good friend' Rory Honeysett would, for a period of forty-eight hours, serve as the repository of the Tocsin Hills mining company's gold shipment to the value of $100,000.

How could a man not feel eight feet tall

and bulletproof with that sort of prospect beckoning?

Yet even at this high moment this heavyweight playmaker of the con, the take and the big grab, found himself beginning to sweat a little.

And he was no longer grinning as he thought ... one hundred grand!

He shook his head. He was so skilled in the art of separating people from their wealth by devious means, he'd never spent a single night behind bars. He'd had accomplices shot out from under him; had experienced more close shaves than he cared to remember. But somehow Nate Wylder always survived and 'most always came out richer than on going in.

But he'd never aimed this high. Nothing like it. He knew jewel-importers who would enlist a dozen hardmen to protect goods worth a measly two to three thousand. What sort of massive security might a man expect to encounter trying to prevent him getting his hands on a prize this size? His cigar had gone out. He flung it away and sought to reassure himself by making a quick appraisal of the talent he'd assembled for Operation Gold-dust.

Seated directly in back of him, Hancock was reassuringly massive and relatively anonymous-looking in the everyday rig of a poorly paid shipping-clerk or doorman. Hancock represented the muscle he might well need, a brute who did as he was told.

Harry Brown, chewing on his fingernails at the big bruiser's side, had the appearance of an unemployed undertaker. The little man was meek, nervous, scared of everything – and the greatest safe-cracker Wylder had ever met.

He frowned as his eyes met those of the third string to his troupe. Conway Stack was dressed like a gentleman's gentleman in rusty dark coat and pants and hard-hitter hat as he sat scanning a newspaper article on a bloody clash between the law and the Bannerman gang in adjacent Bleak County recently.

Wylder shook his head. You could tog this small slender man with the bullet eyes in a clown suit, big feet and all, and most likely he'd still look like a shootist.

'What, boss?' Stack queried in response to his look.

Wylder sighed. 'Try and look inoffensive, will you, Stack? You know, harmless?'

'I thought I was.' The gunman tapped his newspaper. 'What do you make of this Bannerman thing here, boss?'

Wylder made no response, not to be diverted from his thoughts and his driving.

Within minutes the party was offloading in the spacious rear yard of the Federation Hotel on Ojibway Street, Buffalo Horn's finest. The manager remembered Wylder from his previous visit, and he extravagantly tipped the porter who toted his luggage up to the presidential suite while Stack, Brown and Hancock found their own way to the ground-floor room all three would share at the far end of the corridor.

The trio only took long enough to deposit

their bags before hitting the streets to grab a beer and get their ears to the ground. Upstairs, Wylder luxuriated in a foam bath for a full hour, enjoyed a solitary but splendid dinner in his suite then dressed carefully in what was likely the most expensive and discreetly fashionable broadcloth suit frontier-town Buffalo Horn had ever seen.

He stood before the floor-length mirror. His impressive appearance was his stock-in-trade, and he knew it. Looks, charm and a mind like a rattler had enabled him to live far above the poverty line all his life.

Blessed with an actor's chiselled features and fine physique, Wylder was vain as a peacock and relied upon his appearance and charm to camouflage his other dominant characteristic: total and murderous ruthlessness when the chips were down.

Right at this relaxed moment, however, he wasn't feeling either vain or dangerous, just very romantic as he posed and smiled in the glass and allowed his mind to run away from the serious business that had brought him here.

Now he thought of the girl.

A year ago, when he'd last visited, and was guest at the Honeysett home on several occasions, she had been but sixteen years of age, yet already the most remarkable and exciting young woman he'd ever met.

Della Honeysett. She'd be seventeen to eighteen now. He leaned close to the mirror. Could a thirty-two year old swindler-crook realistically expect anyone that age to take him seriously?

Damn right he could!

En route to the door, he paused to glance through at the master bedroom. He licked his lips. What he was thinking and planning would only make his stay in this man's town doubly dangerous, he fully realized. But if you didn't live on the edge, why live at all!

He quit the suite exuding confidence. Collecting Stack from the joint next door, he took himself off for a promenade along the central block beneath the yellow Rager lamps and a summer sky festooned with early stars.

And felt his pulsebeat quicken when he paused before Bob's Cowboy Store to stare across at the imposing façade of Honeysett's fat bank.

He felt like a Crusader dispatched to the Holy Land to tear the Holy Grail from the foul and tainted hands of the unbelievers.

The table boss at the Rough Cut remembered him and found him a seat at the poker layout where, over a period of an hour or so, he managed both to let everyone know Nate Wylder was back in town and win $300, one hundred of which he handed to the table boss as they left.

He read his win as a good omen, was wondering if it was too late to call on Honeysett as they threaded through the crowds on the walks. He was about to swing into the tobacco-seller's for cigars when he noticed a fancy-looking buggy rolling by, and stopped on a dime.

The pair in the buggy were both young, the man slim and sun-bronzed with a look about him that both Wylder and Stack recognized all too readily. But it was the young woman who caught the eye. She was so vibrantly beautiful and animated that she seemed to actually glow as she gazed by the man at her side as though he was the only other person on the street, maybe in all South Dakota.

It was her.

As the rig rolled from sight, Stack turned to look at his employer, paled.

'Boss, what's wrong? You look sick of a sudden.'

Wylder was forced to clear his throat twice before he could speak. Seeing her was unexpected. Seeing her with another man was of course something he should have logically expected. But he wasn't being logical at that moment. Anything but.

'Did ... did you see that girl, Stack?'

'A man'd have to be blind not to. What about her?'

Without responding, Wylder turned and led the way through the nearest set of swinging doors. After a double he was calmer but scarcely felt any better. He drew the bar-keep's attention, and asked:

'Miss Della Honeysett, buddy. She not married by any chance, is she?'

'No, she ain't, sir.'

'I ... I just saw her with a man...'

'Guess that'd be the troublemaker.'

Carefully Wylder lay a five-spot on the bar top. 'Tell me about your troublemaker...'

Later, they quit the saloon and made their way to Chinnick's. They walked slowly. Wylder was busy absorbing everything he'd just been told about what sounded like a lightning romance between 'his' girl of at least some of his dreams, and some kind of mystery man nobody seemed to know anything about other than that he was different and tough. Real tough.

At Chinnick's he was warmly welcomed by Old Bo Fleet and young Jim Easy, both of whom he'd befriended during his prior visit.

Within fifteen minutes Nate Wylder was the center of a laughing, affable crowd of townsmen at the long bar. Easy's group, some of whom he vaguely remembered, gathered around as did the girls and some big spenders – as Wylder turned on the charm. He was at center stage, and this was exactly the kind of situation he revelled in.

Tonight he was a humorist, a supplier-of-news and a first-rate storyteller who could slip into the role of the sober and successful businessman with equal ease and conviction.

He was first with his money on the bar, quickest with the quip and repartee. But he was also a good listener and as time went by he encouraged his new friends to speak more and more freely about themselves and the town, information he absorbed and filed away, not knowing what he might discard or what might prove valuable before he was through here.

This was the criminal hard at work, single-minded, professional, as sure-footed as a catamount, trawling for information, missing nothing and absorbing impressions as he went. Before he was through he sensed the citizenry of Buffalo Horn were vaguely aware that there could be something big afoot in their town, even if they lacked any real notion on what it might be.

He'd like to be a fly on the wall here at Chinnick's around Monday morning when they found out.

Conway Stack eased away from his employer to the wheel when reassured no danger to his boss lurked here in the best-run place in town.

After a time, Hancock and Brown arrived to join him, the pair offering an almost comical contrast to each other, with the former looking somehow larger than ever in these suave surroundings, Harry Brown as colorless and forgettable as a ferret at a skunk convention, his hugely talented fingers tucked away in the pockets of a drab gray jacket.

'Pick up anythin'?' Stack murmured.

'Sure,' grunted Hancock, leaning on the bar. 'This town's wound up. Dunno if they know about the shipment, but it seems they don't.'

'Nate'll find out.' Brown sounded sure. 'Hello, who's this coming in?'

It was Rory Honeysett and his entourage who came surging through the batwings, and Wylder noticed them sooner than anybody. Immediately abandoning his new friends, he thrust his way through the throng and claimed his 'old buddy' with a hug and a handshake.

The banker appeared dazed for a moment, for he'd arrived in a fine temper over something that had occurred at the house, had come to Chinnick's in dire need of a few stiff ones. Yet he was genuinely pleased to see Wylder, who had made a big impression during his earlier visit, and within no time at all the two men had moved off to one side to a quiet alcove flanked by the banker's body-guards. There, Wylder immediately set about softening the other up, employing just the right blend of affability and serious concern to encourage the rich man to confide what was troubling him – he could see plainly that something sure was.

'Well, matter of fact I have been carrying more than my fair load of concerns lately, Nate; this week more than ever. But I'm not sure I can tell you more than that–'

'I was right then,' the other cut in. 'Soon as I saw you come through the doors, I said – there's my old friend Rory, and he's troubled some.' He leaned back and spread his hands, his handsome face as open and innocent as a field of bluebonnets. 'Well, here I am, old friend. Look, it's difficult to open up to folks you know too well, who see you every day. But you're talking to a man who's here today and gone tomorrow. You know me, old friend. Unburden yourself.'

A vaguely confused Rory Honeysett was beginning to feel they really were old intimate friends. And surely there was no overreaching reason why he couldn't confide in a man of this warmth, character and quality?

'Hey, am I being slow on the uptake?' Wylder said suddenly, reaching for his bulging billfold. 'Nine times out of ten when

I meet a man with troubles, it turns out to be money troubles.' He flicked open the billfold and dropped his voice to a confidential level. 'Something to tide you over, maybe, Rory?'

'No, it's not money, Nate. Business has never been better. But I do have a lot on my mind' He paused to study the face before him. It radiated character, concern, integrity. He grappled with himself for a moment longer, then drained his glass and set it down. 'You're right, you know. I do need to off-load to someone...'

He waved a hand at the offer of another and leaned closer.

'The truth of it is, I'm expecting a large gold shipment here on Friday night, Nate. Biggest we've ever handled as a matter of fact. I'll be holding it in my vaults until the soldiers from Fort Slim come for it Monday morning.'

Wylder felt his flesh tingle. 'You set up to handle something that big, Rory? I'm talking security, of course.'

The banker nodded. 'Absolutely secure – no risk about that. But there's another matter, personal, so it is. But then, a man like yourself could hardly be interested in such things...'

'Try me, Rory.'

That was all the encouragement rich Rory needed to unburden himself about his youngest daughter and the rebellious, mad-cap fling she was having with some nobody from noplace.

His companion hung onto every word. Wylder was acutely aware that this self-important man of affairs held the keys to the two things he wanted and meant to have. The gold, of course. And in his typical greedy way, he was equally determined to have the girl – even if for just one night.

Both men had had several drinks by this time. Nate Wylder didn't have time to take things slowly. He threw an arm around Honeysett's shoulders and spoke to him man to man.

'I'm honoured you should see fit to confide

in me, Rory, I surely am. I have to say that, being a simple businessman I probably can't assist you with your big shipment problems – although you probably don't need any help there. But this saddle tramp you describe, he might be right up my alley.'

'What do you mean?'

Wylder shrugged. 'You know how it is, Rory. A man like myself has to be able to take care of himself, and this as often as not means knowing how to deal with trouble-makers and hardcases like this Shannon fellow. My men, Hancock and Stack, are my bodyguards and troubleshooters, and damn good at what they do. Let me–'

'No, Nate, no. I appreciate your concern, but this is a personal matter. There's no call for you to become involved.'

Wylder let it go at that. He knew when to go in hard, when to hold back. They rejoined the crowd at the bar where the original half-dozen drinkers had swollen to a score or more, and were keeping the bartenders hopping. On joining the group,

Wylder and Honeysett took turns treating. Everyone was getting liquored up, with only Stack, Hancock and Brown nursing their drinks. They weren't in this man's town to get drunk or have fun – far from it.

Outside in Front Street a cavalcade of freighters laden with trade goods bound for the north rumbled past, blotting out the voices for a time with the crunch of iron-shod wheels, dust motes wafting through open windows under green-shaded lights.

Most of the party was turned towards the batwings, frowning with annoyance at the racket and dust. So it was that most everybody witnessed the supple-hipped entry of the man who, in one way or another, had been the main topic of conversation around Buffalo Horn for the second day running.

Shannon half-paused, glancing left and right. Then he came casually down to an empty section of the bar, tapped a silver dollar on the zinc-top and said;

'A glass of mineral water, barkeep.'

CHAPTER 4

TROUBLE AT CHINNICK'S

Shannon stood at the long mahogany bar of Chinnick's saloon, his muscular back leaning against the counter edge, one boot heel hooked over the brass footrail, the glass of clear mineral water untouched beside him. His hat was tilted back off his forehead. There was just the hint of a smile at the corners of his mouth as his lazy blue eyes went over the watching faces, clear as glass.

The piano rattled on, for the player's instructions were to keep the music going, especially if there looked like trouble erupting. And if the tense atmosphere that suddenly had gripped the room was anything to go by, that could well be the case.

Honeysett cleared his throat noisily in the

silence while Shannon's eyes ran over Wylder and the three men at his side. The quiet in the big, smoke-hazed room now was too deep to be anything but unnatural.

Behind his long bar, Old Bo Fleet stood motionless and alert. Nobody was buying any longer. He studied Honeysett and Wylder then cut his gaze back to Shannon. He wasn't taken in by the young man's seeming nonchalance. He recalled that he'd looked pretty much the same the previous day mere moments before hammering the troublemaker Reb the length of the bar.

Honeysett set his glass down and approached the man standing alone.

'I was hoping to see you some time today, young man,' he said in his best banker's manner.

'Uh huh,' Shannon grunted.

'It's about—'

'I know what it's about, Mr Honeysett,' Shannon cut in. 'Everybody knows. But you're wastin' your time, man.'

The banker's face hardened. 'You won't

listen to reason, then?'

'I don't see much reason around this town.'

'I won't bandy words with you, mister. You were out with my daughter again today.'

'That's so. We're goin' out tomorrow, too.'

Honeysett shook his head. 'No, I'm afraid not.'

Shannon stood up straight, eyes hard. 'Look, Honeysett, I don't mean you any trouble, but don't lean on me, man. If there's one thing I don't like it's bein' leaned on.'

This brought swift reaction from the bank guards who'd accompanied Honeysett to the saloon. The pair quickly moved up to their employer, flanking him on either side. Wylder, sensing the time was ripe to intervene, gave the nod to his own trio and moved to join them.

Shannon flicked the four a sharp glance. He said to Honeysett in his half-whispering voice:

'These your boys too, banker man?'

'If they have to be, Shannon,' Honeysett replied evenly. 'That's up to you.'

'Trouble here, Rory?' Wylder asked blandly, studying Shannon carefully.

'Who the hell are you?' Brazos demanded.

Wylder frowned. 'I don't like your tone, boy–'

'Easy now, Nate,' Honeysett said placatingly.

But Wylder was looking for an excuse to buy in. He said flatly, 'My name's Nate Wylder. You can call me Mr Wylder.'

'You got a stake in this game, Wylder?' Shannon challenged.

Wylder hooked thumbs in vest pockets, threw his head back challengingly. 'Mr Honeysett is a friend of mine – that gives me all the stake I need.'

'Not in my book, it doesn't. I don't know who you are, mister, and I couldn't give a damn less. But you're buyin' into somethin' that doesn't concern you. So you'd better whistle in your stooges and back off.'

There was such assurance in the way he

spoke, such an air of fearlessness surrounding him, that both Honeysett and Wylder were momentarily nonplussed. Here they were, presenting a united front of seven men, yet this loner was acting as though it was he, not they, who was calling the shots. The bank guards, rugged individuals by home-town standards, also felt the icy threat of blue eyes and hesitated, waiting for direction.

It was ox-shouldered Matt Hancock, anger flushing his cheekbones, who picked up the gauntlet.

'What did you call us, mister?' he demanded in a rumbling voice. 'Stooges?'

'Right.'

Hancock moved in with the muscular assurance of a street-fighter. Two steps separated him from the man by the bar. He covered one of them in a stride, then stopped dead, his head ringing like a gong.

It was several dazed seconds before Wylder's bruiser realized he'd been punched to the jaw, as hard as he could remember and surely faster than he'd ever seen.

He shook his shaggy head, spat blood sideways and swung a mighty haymaker intended to end the dust-up right then and there.

Shannon went under the whistling fist and straightened holding a Colt. There followed the sickening crunch of metal on bone as the steel barrel lashed across Hancock's temple. He staggered and began to fall, eyes rolling in their sockets. As his knees hit the floor with a thud that rattled the glassware, Shannon swayed in and the whistling revolver again slammed home.

Matt Hancock stretched his length amongst the butts and sawdust.

By the time the stunned onlookers could drag their eyes away from Hancock, whose right foot was quivering and stuttering against the floorboards, Shannon's gun was housed again. His elbow was on the bar as he sipped his mineral water. But now his eye was on Conway Stack, whom he'd instantly identified as the one to watch in the bunch. But Stack had sized him up in return, and kept his hands well away from his gun. For now.

Blue eyes flicked at Honeysett and Wylder. But there was no danger. Honeysett was a physical coward, while Wylder mostly hired men to hurt people for him. Right now, each felt he was standing too close to the sort of unpredictable danger they always tried to avoid.

For that pregnant moment, Shannon stood in unchallenged command beneath the hanging lamps which were still swaying slightly from the impact of big Hancock's mighty fall.

'Keep the change, old-timer,' he murmured to an open-mouthed Old Bo, then sauntered out, bootheels loud in the quiet.

Front Street was quiet with only the odd walker to be seen. There was a welcoming breeze coming in from the south, clearing the eternal dust and stirring the carefully tended trees lining both sides of the street.

Shannon went to the hitch rail and swung up on the high-shouldered and mean-eyed roan. The animal tried to bite him and skittered backwards into the center of the street. Shannon controlled the animal effortlessly and sat for a moment staring at Chinnick's.

Then he gigged the gelding westward.

He followed the street its full length before heading for a disused old trail that climbed northwest into the high country. It was instinctive for him to hip around in his saddle several times to see if he was being followed. But the trail behind lay empty, as was the one ahead: a faint yellow ribbon of rising road which within a few miles was swallowed in the tracklessness of Sawteeth Range's most desolate regions.

It was the Feast of the Assumption and the Honeysett girls were on their way to Mass down on Church Street where the Catholic, Baptist and Lutheran houses of worship all stood together in ecumenical harmony beneath the flame trees.

The day was bright and there was a

bounce in the girls' step as they swung into Front and made their way past the billiard parlor and Abbey's Dress-shop.

Milly slowed to look longingly at the new gowns on display but Della tugged her by the sleeve and they didn't stop. None of the sisters was particularly spiritual, it was true, but when Grandma Clara announced a young woman was going to Mass it meant she was going, like it or not.

But there were compensations. The old lady had slept late this morning, and as a consequence all had been able to quit the house sporting their latest finery, whereas had Grandma been on deck they'd be making their way across the main street right now in sober navy-blues and dark stockings, complete with hats and veils.

The town was not fully awake as yet and there was a fresh bright look about the main street, which the water-carter had travelled along a short time earlier on the first of his many journeys of the day, laying the eternal dust of Buffalo Horn.

Shirleen waved to her current boyfriend as he leaned from a hotel window with a towel round his neck, and Cassie suppressed a giggle when they sighted sober Sheriff Bean dodging the snapping teeth of a young horse he was leading down the lane by the jailhouse half a block distant.

Pleased with just about everything this bright morning, themselves especially, the Honeysett sisters were mounting the plankwalk by the Rough Cut saloon, well aware of the pretty picture they made and chatting animatedly, when Milly suddenly stopped and clapped a hand to her breast with a gasped:

'My God!'

The others stopped.

'What on earth...?' Cassie began half-crossly. Then she too saw the familiar figure strolling along the plankwalk before the gunsmith's, the sun throwing his shadow long and black before him. 'Oh dear,' she sighed, with a quick glance at her youngest sister. 'Honey, perhaps it's best if we go the other way, down the alley.'

'Too late,' Della said, eyes shining the way they always did when he was around. 'He's seen us.' She raised a gloved hand and waved gaily. 'Coming to Mass?' she called.

And Muriel clucked in shock: 'Really, Della Honeysett...'

'I'd surely admire to,' Shannon called back, halting to lean one shoulder against a porch support. 'Only thing, I've just hired a rig to take a run south...' He paused a moment, blue eyes looking at the other three. Then he said, 'Want to come along?'

'No!' Milly said emphatically. But it was already too late. Lifting her skirts out of the dust, Della was already halfway across the street.

'I won't be late!' she called back over her shoulder. 'Tell Papa ... oh, tell him what you like. Bye!'

'Your sisters don't look too pleased,' Shannon smiled as he extended a hand to swing her up onto the high walk at his side. 'Sure you won't get scalped or horsewhipped?'

She swept off her hat and smiled radiantly. 'Where are we going?'

'Good girl,' he said, and took her elbow just like a real gentleman. They vanished down Tuckett's Lane leading to the Bright's Livery and Grain Barn. The rig they hired was a fancy buggy with ample space under the sides of the seat for the rubber-tyred, brass-rimmed wheels to turn with a real flourish. It boasted yellow spokes with brass lamps and a matching canvas top which could be rolled back in mild weather.

Had there been any chance of the couple at the center of Buffalo Horn's hottest gossip topic slipping away from town unnoticed, it was dashed by the eye-catching rig that spanked off down the south road minutes later drawn by a blood-red bay, attracting every eye.

Not that this seemed to bother either of the two onboard.

'Where are we going?' Della asked as the last of the houses fell behind.

'Do you need to know?'

'Of course not.'

'Good. Sometimes it's best not to know where you are headin'. You just go!'

It was a twenty-minute run down to the remote Deuces trailhouse. Already there were horses tethered outside with a rig or two parked in back. Della couldn't wait to be handed down and escorted inside. The Deuces had the reputation as a wild place and needless to say no Honeysett female was allowed to set foot inside.

With blinds drawn against the heat the saloon-cum-gambling-hall-cum-hangout for the footloose and fancy-free was invitingly cool and shadowed inside. It smelt good and there was music from a three-man cowboy combo in the far corner. Further, it seemed none of the lonelies, drifters, painted women or bar staff seemed to find anything unusual about the daughter of the richest man in the district showing up unannounced.

This would have put the girl at her ease, had she needed it. But she didn't. She was totally confident in any situation, and even had that been otherwise his company would have made her so.

A swarthy barkeep with a polka-dot bandanna knotted around his head greeted Shannon by name, nodded gravely to the girl.

'Stayin' over, drinkin', dancin' or all three, Shannon?'

'You mightn't believe it,' Shannon smiled at her, 'but I was headin' down here to do a little dancin' today.' He indicated the two couples already gliding round the waxed floor to strains of a Mexican love-song. 'There's noplace a man can dance in the middle of the day in your town.'

Della's laughter tinkled through the saloon. He was crazy, she was thinking. Yet the more she gazed about and absorbed the ambience of this place the more she began to feel it mightn't be so crazy after all. These people here looked normal enough – and why not dance in the middle of the day anyway? The whole idea appealed to her.

She'd always loved saloons, hence her visits to Chinnick's. She found saloon folk less serious, somehow freer, and she loved freedom more than life. Freedom from responsibility, boredom, respectability, repression. Freedom to be oneself. She'd always sought the latter and as a consequence had always been in trouble of one kind or another.

She slid from the stool and linked her arms about his neck. He grabbed her with a whispery laugh and they glided out onto the floor.

For Della, the hours blurred by in a whirl of pleasure, easy company, a wonderful feeling of time standing still. It was mid-afternoon before they quit the trailhouse; he had something else he wanted her to see before darkdown.

She expected they'd take the north trail back for town but instead he found a rough climbing-track a mile from the trailhouse, which they followed westwards through thinning timber country, with the jagged gray backbone of the Sawteeth Range looming higher and closer as they climbed.

Della just sat back in her cushioned seat watching both him and the rugged mountain scenery, and never once allowed her thoughts to dwell on Buffalo Horn or what might await her on her return.

All her life she'd dreamed of something like this happening to her: the man unlike all other men coming into her life, sweeping her off her feet, not questioning her or being questioned. She knew she wasn't being practical, didn't know if this would continue for an hour or a lifetime. Didn't want to know. Just wanted today to go on forever.

She wasn't sure how they reached the high valley with the long yellow grass rippling in the wind and great stone formations shaped like primitive gods casting immense fingers of shadow under a low slanting sun.

They walked to a vast rock ledge the size of a field where they sat in silence, the wind blowing off the Sawteeth tossing her hair, his eyes blue as china when he smiled at her.

No explanations. No questions. They just sat there until Della turned her head at a faint sound from the south, like drums.

Moments later they were there, the wild-horse bunch seeming to sail through the sea of belly-high grass, heads up, eyes glinting fire, eating distance with their tireless fluent stride – the essence of the wilderness encapsulated in the exhilarating form of fifty untamed broomtails streaming by without a glance in the direction of the two man-things on the rock slab. Running for no reason, or running for sheer joy, what did it matter. It was a sight to fire the blood and to cause a young girl to wonder how she had been able to endure being caged for sixteen long years.

It was dark before they cleared the range, and they could see the glow of the lights long before the actual town came into sight.

At last she spoke. 'Why did you take me to see the horses?'

'I reckoned you needed to see them, is all.'

'Do you go there often?'

'Mostly I just go ... you know?'

'Will … will you go from here one day?'

'Guess I'll know when one day comes.'

She didn't really understand him, she mused, leaning her head against his shoulder. Not in the conventional sense, at least. But on another level she seemed to understand him better than anybody she'd ever known, and he her.

She knew she loved him. And prayed she would find the strength to survive when he left her, as everybody warned he surely would.

CHAPTER 5

WHERE GUN WOLVES GATHER

Reece Bannerman stood before the mouth of the cave, squinting out over the broken, tumbledown landscape of Wild Horse Bluffs. His narrowed eyes followed the smooth, leisurely passage of a battered old eagle, gliding high upon the late afternoon thermals. He drew the thin Mexican stogie from between his teeth, spat unerringly at a curious lizard which had thrust its head out from beneath a slab of rock twenty feet away. He chuckled as the reptile scuttled out of range.

From the cavern in back of him, a voice said sourly, 'Wish I could find somethin' funny in this hell-hole.'

Bannerman grinned back into the gloom of the cave where the dim shapes of men could be seen.

'What's the matter, Blazer?' he called. 'Losing your sense of humor?'

There was a disgusted growl, the scrape of metal against rock, and Bannerman was joined by a black-bearded outlaw toting a rifle. Joe Blazer scowled in disgust at the tumbling, tawny landscape.

'Don't it never rain up here?' he complained.

'What you need is coffee,' Bannerman

diagnosed. 'Reckon we could all handle a little good joe, come to that. Why not put some on the fire, huh?'

Blazer stared at his leader sourly, then slouched off down the short slope fronting the cave to where a discreet little fire burned in a rocky alcove.

Bannerman shoved the cigar back between powerful teeth and grinned around it.

Standing there before the dark cavern-mouth that pocked this broken-down old cliff face, his trail rig still showing traces of alkali from the Bleak County canyon country which lay beyond the jagged fangs of the Sawteeth chopping the skies, Reece Bannerman appeared wild enough for anything, and maybe impressive enough to measure up to the legend that had surrounded him during his lifetime on the owlhoot.

A Herculean figure with a great head of red-gold hair and curly blond beard, there was about this man an air of violence and directionless determination. He was at once superficially genial, ruthless and quick-witted. His life on the dodge was characterized by genuine acts of tenderness and humanity contrasted with even more memorable episodes of mindless savagery.

Today, his mood was good for reasons his henchmen were as yet not privy to. His fierce and ugly countenance was a mask of concentration as he drew a .44 and broke it open. He was squinting down the dark mirror-shine of the barrel as his henchmen emerged, responding to the smell of hot coffee.

One man was short and wide-shouldered with a hard-boned, expressionless face. Chav Cody walked with a limp, a legacy of the gang's clash with an Army detail outside the Indian camp at Badlanders River. The other, knuckling sleep from his eyes, was tall and heavily built with a sullen face that showed traces of recent violence. Reb Houston appeared seriously out of sorts.

'Where is he?' he grumped, squinting around.

'Who?' Bannerman asked.

'The new man.' Houston fingered a badly bruised jaw. 'Your new man, that is.'

Bannerman blew a gust of tobacco smoke into the pristine high country air.

'Yeah, he stopped by just like he said he would,' he said easily, ignoring the other's venom.

'And?'

'Everythin's goin' like clockwork. The shipment's due in Friday afternoon at four o'clock with a ten-man escort from the mine. It'll be held there in the vaults until Monday mornin'. Under bank security. This Honeysett figures the less fuss he makes the less likely anybody's gonna suspect what he's holdin', hey, hey.'

'We knew all that before, thanks to Marty,' Houston pointed out. He shook his woolly head. 'Poor old Marty...'

'Poor Marty' indeed. Isaac Martin was the former gang member who'd first stumbled upon the news of the great shipment quite by accident thanks to an unsuspecting kinsman, a security guard from the Tocsin Hills mine, who'd let the information slip during a drunken family get-together.

It was this news that had prompted the bunch to stage their successful gunsmoke breakout from Bleak County and make the Sawteeth crossing into Bright's. Only thing, Poor Marty had been gunned down by the possemen down at Twelve Canyons and would never get to see his pards make a grab for the biggest payday of their thieving lives.

'Forget Marty,' Bannerman said shortly. 'And forget belly-aching about the new guy while you're at it. I gave you your chance down in the town and you screwed it up, Reb. But he's doin' a good job.'

The rank-and-filers began wrangling amongst themselves. Keeping them from going for one another's throats was the leader's toughest task during these waiting days in the wilds. Heat, inaction and solitude was wearing everybody thin.

'Reckon that coffee ought to be ready by now.'

The others hesitated, then followed him downslope, boots sinking in pockets of powdery dust. The full heat of the sun struck hard after the cliff shade even though it was late in the day with the shadows of buttes and spires forming weird spidery designs upon the burning earth. Bannerman gazed up at the sky. The old eagle was gone. There would be few pickings 'way up here.

Tethered horses gazed at them beneath a rock shelf as they reached the fire. Horseflesh had taken a beating in that brutal climb up the stark west face of the Sawteeth. Beyond the horse shelter, Blazer looked up from the fire sulkily.

'It's ready,' he grumped. 'Help yourselves.'

Nobody spoke again until they'd taken their first reviving draughts from battered pannikins. There was something about hot coffee that took the edge off a man's temper, even tetchy and dangerous tempers like theirs.

One by one they found themselves shady spots to hunker down. Fingers got busy with papers and tobacco, eyes sought out the horses and each man noted the condition of his own mount, for the horses were their life's blood. Then they gazed up at the vast bleached curve of the sky and felt the faintest hint of a breeze. Woodsmoke, coffee and good tobacco were already doing their healing work.

Soon the boys were yarning amongst themselves, which suited Bannerman fine. He was the thinking arm of this outfit, and Reb Houston had got him thinking about the new man he'd enlisted to compensate for his loss down at Twelve Canyons.

The recruit was an impressive fellow, and was reporting back both on time and intelligently. If only he was less sure of himself, Bannerman brooded, more sociable. That young rooster was easy to respect but hard to get to know...

'Boss!' called Cody.

'What?'

'How about giving us the rest of the news from town?'

'I said there was no news.'

'That's what you said.'

Bannerman was ready to snap a retort, but held his tongue. He and Cody had ridden the river together long enough almost to know what the other was thinking. Besides, there was no need to keep secret about anything at this late stage of the game.

'Nate Wylder's in town,' he stated quietly.

Cody whistled low through his teeth. But both Blazer and Houston traded blank looks, then looked across at Bannerman.

'Who's Wylder?' Blazer demanded. 'Law?'

'Who's Wylder?' Bannerman repeated reflectively. 'That's a mighty good question, *amigos*.'

'What's he doin' in Buffalo Horn?' Cody asked sharply.

'Livin' it up big. Booked in at the Federation Hotel. Playin' the part of an exporter this time round.'

'Exporter!' snorted Cody, massaging his heavy jaw. 'Last time I cut Nate Wylder's trail in a little burg outside Austin, he was a representative for an Eastern bank. That damned fraudster!' A pause. 'Fraudster, but no bastard to trifle with, that's for sure and free.'

Reb Houston seemed about to mash his stove-up old coffee pannikin in his big hairy hands.

'Well, keep the big secret to yourselves, why don't you?'

Bannerman tossed the dregs of his coffee into the dust with a grin.

'No secret, pards. It's just that Chav and me ain't all that sure what this geezer is ourselves.'

'Me and Reece have cut his trail once or twice over the past couple years,' Cody proffered in response to the deepening perplexity of both Blazer and Houston. 'At first we thought he really was big business–'

'We even thought about lightenin' his roll for him,' Bannerman interrupted with a chuckle.

'That's a fact,' Cody went on. 'Could be just as well we didn't try it. You see, in this town out in Idaho, there was another bunch of thieves like me and Reece, and they tangled with Wylder over some deal.' He spread his hands. 'Turned out Wylder wasn't on his lonesome, like we figured. When this bunch went after Wylder, his bunch showed up and shot 'em to doll rags. We found out later Wylder most always travels with a pack. This time there was five fellers with him, and two of 'em were gunsharks that done most of the killin' that day.'

'He's owlhoot?' Houston asked.

Bannerman shrugged. 'Who knows?'

'What he is, is a real smart operator,' supplied Chav Cody. 'We still don't know for sure just what brand he wears, but the whisper is he's a scam artist and always plays to win. Thinks big too, so I'm told.'

'Mebbe he really is just a businessman?' speculated a sceptical Houston. 'You know, one of those guys who just likes to have a couple guns handy in case things go wrong.'

Bannerman stood, running fingers through his splendid red-gold thatch, a habitual gesture.

'One story we heard that seemed to have some weight was about a train hold-up in Mexico around last Christmas. Seemed Wylder was havin' a run of outs with the con game and needed *dinero* in the worst way. So he planned to stick up this here train. He put ten men on his payroll and even toted a gun himself, somethin' he don't like to do normally. They got off with ten grand and left three Mexes dead. This joker who told us the story claimed he was in on the job, and had a fat wad of cash as proof ... so the story could be true.'

'Had a fat wad until you and me met up with him, you mean,' Cody said with a twinkle in his eye.

Bannerman and Cody slapped their knees and laughed deep in their bellies at the recollection of a past success. But neither of their saddle pards was satisfied. Both Blazer and Houston were hard and humourless denizens of the owlhoot. They were hoping to get rich down in Buffalo Horn and were prepared to risk life and limb to get their hands on a king's ransom in yellow gold.

But they weren't fools.

Any lone rider who chanced his arm on a major job without learning everything there was to be known about the risks, was seen as six kinds of a fool.

The gang already had concrete plans on how to crack the bank and deal with its security, but knew it would still be a high-risk undertaking. If by chance this Wylder and his outfit might be looking for a slice of the same pie, they needed to know about it. Now.

Houston started to say as much but Bannerman shut him up with a curt gesture. The leader was a wild man with a short fuse so they knew better than to push a thing when he got that glitter in his eye.

'Our new scout's checkin' Wylder out right now,' he stated with an air of finality. 'We'll wait until he reports back until we start in shyin' at shadows.'

'Seems to me Reece is settin' a heap of

store by this new joker he recruited,' Blazer opined later as he and Houston tended the horses.

'Yeah, you'd think he was a real wonder.' Houston turned and spat. 'Me? I wouldn't trust him out of sight. How can you trust any pilgrim when you can't even tell what's goin' on behind his eyes, or what he's thinkin' even?'

'Mebbe you worry too much, Reb.'

'And mebbe you don't worry enough, rumdum.'

They finished the chore in silence. Pacing slowly to and fro outside, Bannerman reflected that the weekend had better arrive in a hurry before they got to fighting amongst themselves up here. But they'd better think twice before they started anything. He wanted that Tocsin gold so bad he could taste it, and nothing or nobody was going to spoil his chance of getting it.

CHAPTER 6

THE HUNGRY ONES

The rays of the lowering sun seemed to linger strongest upon the figures of the man and the horse standing statue-still side by side upon a huge granite outcropping watching the long day burning away towards evening.

From a nearby draw snaked a little cooling breath of wind from the high country which feathered the roan's long tail causing it to brush against Shannon's shoulder.

The man didn't seem to notice. He continued to stand there, erect and expressionless with all movement suspended, the brass cartridge rims in his gunbelt winking in the light. He could have been a holy man experiencing some kind of revelation, so intense was his concentration, when in reality he was merely considering the simplest and most basic of choices.

Go or stay.

Fork leather and simply vanish into the coming night as he'd done so many times before in his vagabond life, then just keep riding until he'd ridden far enough. Taste again the total freedom that he'd sought, found and revelled in ever since a tousle-headed kid in short britches first took up a gun and discovered that freedom was something anybody could achieve and hold only if he was strong enough.

Head west or return to the town tonight?

The horse nudged him with its long ugly nose. The animal just wanted to run; it didn't much care where.

'Easy,' Shannon muttered perfunctorily as the red disc vanished behind a cloud, bringing shadows rushing across the Dakota lands swifter than the eye could follow.

Decision time.

Every instinct warned him to cut adrift

before the slow unfolding drama of Buffalo Horn in which he was playing a vital part reached a climax. Get gone before hell erupted and left the scattered dead all littering the townscape. Reasoning against this temptation to run was one single voice, but it was her voice.

He seemed to shiver.

He was twenty-two years of age and had never really cared for any woman until now, and she just a girl, yet a girl like no other.

That night he was expected at the grand house on Cedar Street for what Della described as a little get-together of friends and some interesting people. He suspected that if he should attend he might well be the odd man out, the target of all those well-heeled and educated 'friends and interesting people' who would just love to have somebody who'd caused their host so much *Angst* in recent days at their mercy.

He glanced back upslope to where the roof of a rude cabin showed through the trees. He'd just spent a leisurely hour with two greenhorn fossickers who until recently had worked for the Honeysett Bank. He'd secured information which he would in turn pass on to the man who was presently hiring his skills and his gun. He was good at what he did, but would quit it in a moment if the impulse took him.

He reined in his thoughts and focused them back on the night ahead.

He would be a fool to go to town, a fool not to run while he still could, said the back of his mind.

Then he told the back of his mind to shut up, and with a sudden grin vaulted into the saddle, kicked once and headed for Buffalo Horn.

She would be there. What else mattered a plug damn?

Nate Wylder adjusted his floral armbands carefully, tugged down the points of his bottle-green vest and moved to catch a glimpse of himself in the hotel room mirror.

Perfect.

The big windows of his suite at the Federation overlooked Front Street where shades were drawn against the late afternoon glare. Wylder could feel the pulsebeat of the approaching evening rising up from bars and stores. It excited him. The night ahead was shaping up as something special on many different levels.

Naturally the bank job dominated his thoughts, and he was readying to move his plans in that direction significantly forward right now.

That would be the business part of the hours ahead. The other was the party at the Honeysetts. He had big plans for that also, especially if Della's saddle bum was dumb enough to show.

Times like this he saw himself as a winner all the way, and could feel the genial and glad-handing man-about-town persona he had adopted here slowly but surely giving way to the real Wylder who could be as ruthless and brutal as a Jesse James when the chips were down and the game was afoot.

Seated on a pair of straight-backed chairs, Harry Brown and Conway Stack smoked tailor-made cigarettes and followed Wylder's brisk, methodical movements around the room. The fourth member of the bunch, Matt Hancock, was in the room downstairs, still recovering from his pistol-whipping.

Wylder produced a key-ring and unlocked a bureau drawer. He brought out a leather case which he in turn unlocked with another key, then began to take from it one-hundred-dollar bills which he counted as he placed them on the bureau top.

His henchmen stared.

Wylder continued counting.

The gunman got to his feet with a frown.

'Damnit, Nate, I thought you said you were broke.'

Wylder continued counting until at last he grunted: 'Five thousand iron men.' He relocked the case, replaced it in the drawer and stuffed the fat bundle of cash in an inside pocket before glancing up. 'I am broke.'

'Five thousand is broke?' Brown queried owlishly.

'Investment capital,' Wylder replied. 'Somebody get my jacket.'

Then, as Brown meekly got his coat, he added, 'Boys, it's Thursday night, remember? High time we took our first close-up look at that wonderful safe Honeysett never stops bragging about. Right?'

Brown's spaniel eyes immediately lighted up.

'Yeah, the safe. I've been waiting for us to get around to that.'

'Me too,' agreed poker-faced Stack. 'But more to see how you figure goin' about than anythin' else, Nate.'

Wylder looked at his gunman. 'Remind me, Stack. What exactly do we know about Honeysett and his bank right now?'

'Well, we know the shipment is due to arrive tomorrow afternoon around four with an armed escort of ten. We also know the escort will stay on until the gold's locked away, then they'll skeedaddle, leaving just

Honeysett's regular security to watch over the bank until Monday. This is so having a whole bunch of people hanging round the bank won't tip bad asses like us as to what's going on. Honeysett won't be opening his safe until Monday morning when the soldiers from Fort Slim arrive to take escort the rest of the journey.'

'OK.' Wylder's tone was brisk. 'Now, what do we know about this safe, Harry boy?'

Harry Brown had done his homework well, and safes were this miserable little thief's whole life.

'It's a two-ton Cross and Gruber combination safe 1874 model,' he recited. 'It's guaranteed burglar proof by the manufacturers who think enough of their guarantee to back it up with a ten-thousand-dollar warranty. The safe's located in the basement of the bank and is divided from the upstairs section by a door with a straight-out padlock grille – kid's pickings. As far as anybody knows the safe is crackproof, and if this is so then there's nothing I know can crack her.' The little man paused, then added: 'Oh yeah. It's also supposed to be fire-proof, tamper-proof, explosive-proof and–'

'Easy pickings,' Wylder cut in confidently.

'But how...?'

'Combination, Harry boy. That's how.'

Harry Brown goggled. 'You want me to figure the combination of this monster? You've got to be kidding, Nate. You got any notion how many combinations they can have on these things.'

'I know this is so.' Wylder's manner was flippant. Then he sobered. 'Harry boy, you told me once that you can count the fall of tumblers in a combination safe if you just heard them a few times. Is this so?'

'Sure. Like, when someone dials four, it takes longer for the tumblers to mesh than when he dials two. Eight and nine take longer still. It's all only in split seconds, but to an old picker like me it's clear as a big bell. I won a bet like that once, listening to a geezer working his combination, then opening her myself. It's a gift.'

'All right then, sharpen up those jugs of yours,' Wylder said, collecting his stylish hat, 'and leave the rest to me. Conway, you can go have a shot. Harry, you come with me. Get the door somebody.'

On his way out, Wylder paused to glance at his bedroom. Although preoccupied with other matters right now, he found himself standing there with vivid visions of Della Honeysett and that big beautiful bed crowding his thoughts. He couldn't believe the grip that girl exerted over him. At times it seemed he thought more about her than his hundred thousand, which was no way for a big-time player to function. Yet he couldn't deny she captivated him totally, and, Wylder-like, he knew with equal certainty that he would have her, no matter what it took.

Walkers gave way to the pair as they made their way along the plankwalks for the bank with Wylder striding out leading the way with bristling self-assurance until he came to an abrupt halt before the coffee-house.

A mean-eyed roan gelding stood hipshot

at the hitch rail trying to chew up its bridle.

Two strides took him to the front window. The place was crowded but the couple seated over by the rear window stood out like beacons – or at least did so to Nate Wylder's gaze. They sat close together and Della had her hand resting on the drifter's arm.

For just a moment Wylder wished he was toting a gun, so sudden and irrational was his jealousy. Next he wished he'd brought Stack along – the man he'd hired for his gunskill. For a loco moment he was tempted ... but caught hold of himself and turned his back on the window – the black anger slowly draining from his face, leaving him shaking.

This was crazy!

'You OK, boss?' Brown asked anxiously.

Wylder wasn't about to say one word. Instead he just tugged his hat low and led the way on to the bank, where, in no time at all, they were shown into the plush office of the man Wylder had been courting all week. Rory Honeysett greeted him with a beaming of welcome.

'Good to see you, Nate,' the little man beamed. 'All set for tonight?'

'Wouldn't miss it, Rory.' Wylder smiled, accepting a cheroot. 'Appreciate the invitation.'

The banker turned sober for a moment. 'You realize what it's all about, don't you?'

Wylder's handsome features hardened. 'That bum?'

'That bum who has my daughter acting like a bitch in heat – if you'll forgive my language.' Honeysett savagely bit off the tip of his cigar and spat it into a green-painted wastebasket. 'It's a desperate last play on my part to make her see what a witless, probably illiterate saddle tramp and social misfit that boy is, and I can't think of a better way of achieving this than by her having the experience of seeing him in her own home amongst her own kind making six kinds of an ass of himself. Er, what's this, Nate?'

Wylder had dipped into a pocket to produce a package which he handed across with a smile.

'Just a little token ... might make you feel better about that nobody, Rory.'

The gold-plated cigar-case the banker unwrapped gleamed in the light. The inscription read: TO RORY FROM NATE IN APPRECIATION OF YOUR HOS-PITALITY.

Honeysett was charmed and flattered – as he was meant to be. But Wylder soon let the man know he'd also come on business: the matter of a deposit. 'I'm a little nervous about carrying large sums about, Rory,' he confided, drawing the fat wad of notes from an inside pocket. 'Five thousand. Could you take care of this for me for a week or so?'

The banker smiled. 'Why, that's what we're here for. I'll write you your receipt personally, my friend.'

'Ahh ... I guess this will go into your new vault, eh, Rory?' Wylder enquired.

'Why, probably not, Nate.'

'Well, the truth is, that as a businessman who's used to depositing large sums with banks – that five grand is just chicken feed of course – I take a personal interest in all matters of security. I'd surely admire to take a look at your fine safe. Would that be possible?'

'Well, er, I...'

'Of course if you'd rather not...'

'No, no, not at all.' The banker rose and picked up the money. He glanced at Brown. 'Your friend...?'

'He's my accountant, amongst other things, Rory. He'd feel honoured if he could get to see your pride and joy also.'

The banker finally acceded, then apologized when he summoned two heavily armed guards to accompany his two guests as they made their way through the iron grille to the basement.

'No offence taken, Rory,' Wylder assured. 'Matter of fact the more I see of how you run your business the more impressed I become. Ahh, so that's the beauty, is it?'

'It sure is.'

The safe was six feet high by five wide, set solidly in bricks and mortar. It gleamed with expensive newness in the lamplight. On the door were etched the words:

CROSS & GRUBER
SAFEMAKERS
BOSTON
1874

'Well, it looks everything you say, Rory.' Wylder spoke with the right degree of awe. 'Anything in it yet?'

'I'm saving it for the gold.'

'Well, seeing as it's empty, is there any harm in showing us how it opens?'

'Well, er...' Honeysett hesitated, looked at his guards. Then he chuckled. 'Hell no. No harm at all. Fact is, I like to show it off. Of course, I'm the only one who knows the combination. I told you that, didn't I, Nate?'

'Yes. But aren't you afraid of forgetting it?'

'No, it's in my head for keeps. Er, you'll understand if I ask yourself and Mr Brown to remain where you are while I'm working the dial, won't you? You understand?'

'Of course we do. Go right ahead, Rory.'

The banker went to the safe door, shot his cuffs and raised his right hand to the dial, his face a study in concentration, his body shielding his movements from the others in the room.

Wylder and the bank guards watched the man, intrigued. Only Brown appeared uninterested, staring blankly at the cement floor. The little man wasn't hearing the breathing of those around him, the dimmer sounds of activity upstairs. He had blotted them all out, was concentrating exclusively on those smooth, precise mechanical clicks. To his cracksman's ears, each sound held the sweet beauty of the poet's tongue. And in his head, he counted and remembered. A longish pause ... 6 ... a shorter following ... 4 ... and that was ... 6 again ... 5...

CHAPTER 7

TRUE COLORS

Shannon and Della passed through the outsized *zaguán* gates of the Honeysett compound and strolled arm-in-arm along the flagged pathway. They walked close together, his dark head bent attentively to her words, her upturned face catching the glow of the house-lights.

Music tinkled from within as guests' rigs rolled up to halt beneath the giant oaks.

The couple halted at the side porch steps. Shannon, bareheaded and with his hat hanging by its chinstrap from his sixgun handle, said quietly;

'You'd better go in.'

She pouted. 'I don't want to go in.'

'Why not?'

'I want to stay here with you.'

'You've been with me two hours, girl.'

'I want to be with you all the time.'

'Della, I–'

'Stop! You were about to say something serious, weren't you?'

'Sometimes you have to be serious.'

'Not us. Not you and me, Shannon. We're different. Tell me that we're different, that we don't have to go around with long faces and saying solemn boring things all our lives just like everybody else.'

'You're beautiful,' he murmured. 'That's all I was going to say. Beautiful and amazing.'

She pressed his hard brown hand closer against her face, studying him searchingly. 'Why amazing?'

'You've never asked me anythin'. Where I come from what I do – even where I sleep. To me, that's amazing.'

'Would you tell me if I asked?'

'No.'

'Then it's best I don't ask, isn't it?'

He disengaged his hand and turned away to the porch railing, looking back along the pathway towards the gates.

'No, I wouldn't have told you, before. But maybe it's time I did now.'

'I don't want to know.'

He turned sharply. 'Why do you say that?'

She folded her arms, looked down at them. 'No reason. I just don't, is all.'

'Della, we've got close in just a handful of days. Real close. So tell me why you don't want to know more about me.'

'We've been happy, Shannon, happier than I've ever dreamed possible. I just don't want anything to change, not one thing.'

'You think me opening up would change things?'

'It would.'

'How come?'

'You have something that you've wanted to tell me, ever since we met. It must be something very serious. For all I know, you could be married, or an outlaw, or...'

'An outlaw? What makes you say that?'

'Why ... nothing. It's just something I said...'

'What if it's true?'

'I wouldn't care – only if it made you go away from me. Darling, I've lived all my life amongst respectable people, until I'm half-choked with respectability. I've watched Papa robbing poor little farmers blind for years and calling it business. I've met the men he brings here to the house; fat, sleek men who boast about some sharp deal they've just clinched, something that will make somebody suffer. I've seen respectable married men and the way they look at me, heard their respectable wives running their menfolk down to one another. You see, I've been respectable all my life and I wouldn't give you a plugged nickel if I never saw so much as a hint of it again as long as I live.'

She spoke with passion. He smiled, the way he only smiled with her.

'I knew you were different from any girl I'd ever met when I sashayed into Chinnick's and saw you standing up to Houston.'

She put her arms around his waist.

'I know I'm different,' she conceded. 'And it used worry me, once. But not any more. You are different also. You don't fit in – you can't fit. We are misfits, you and I, but I know we are meant to be together.'

Their lips met. For a long space they clung together with fierce urgency, unaware, uncaring. He was the first to break apart.

'You'd better go in, Della.'

'All right. But you will come by later, won't you?'

'The supper? I don't know if I–'

'Please.'

He ran fingers through his crop of dark curls.

'Honey, it doesn't make sense, your old man invitin' me to his shindig. He'd rather I fell in a gopher hole and broke all my legs, than feed me. I smell a set-up about all this. Somethin' just not right.'

'Perhaps he wants to be friends?'

'Your pa and I were born to ride forked trails. I know it and he knows it. There's too much hard money separatin' us for things ever to be different. He's up to somethin'.'

'Afraid?'

'Reckon not.'

'Then if you don't come, I'll believe you are afraid. Please change your mind. I want my sisters and Granny to get to know you better. For me?'

He hesitated only briefly. 'I'll go put on a clean shirt.'

'Nine o'clock,' she reminded as he turned to go.

'I'll be here.'

He disappeared down the pathway. Listening to his hoofbeats fade, she touched her face where he'd kissed her.

'He's a right smart walker, isn't he.'

The voice from the darkened window in back brought Della around with a start.

'Granny!'

She crossed to the window and peered into the dimly lit room to see her grandmother comfortable in her rosewood rocker, smiling smugly.

'There's nothing I enjoy more than a little eavesdropping.'

'Granny, you're hopeless,' Della chided with mock severity. Then, eagerly, 'Well, what do you think of him? Isn't he gorgeous?'

Clara Honeysett, wrinkled, gray, weathered and well beyond her three-score-and-ten, yet bright-eyed and sharp-witted, chuckled.

'Reminds me of your grandfather, missy. Black Sean Honeysett. He had a cocky way of walking and standing just like that. I guess your wild one and Sean would have hit it off just fine.'

Della brushed at her eyes.

'That's about the nicest thing you could have said, Granny. I'm so happy right now...'

'It's not happy you are, my girl, you're in love. Isn't that right?'

Della leaned on the sill and nodded. 'Yes, Granny,' she said simply.

'Well, that's fine. I was married at sixteen myself.'

'But there are so many things – Father

hates Shannon, and the girls all think he's some kind of a hobo. They'll never accept him, I know.'

'Accept? Is this my Della speaking? When did you start caring about acceptance? In any case, I wouldn't fret too much about your father or his feelings. Why, this whole shebang is just a trick to lure your cowboy into his net and then show him up in your eyes as a fool and a nobody before all your fine friends.'

'I suspected that. But Shannon won't make a fool of himself. I've seen him with people, and they like him – most of them. He has fine manners and he's a gentleman.'

'Then you'd best get inside and pretty yourself up for when your fine gentleman comes back.'

Della rushed into the room, kissed the old lady upon the cheek and vanished in a whirl of taffeta. Granny Honeysett started her rocker going again and thought about a young man with hair like a raven's wing who'd swaggered into her life what seemed a hundred years ago. She smiled and looked out over the garden. The moon was just coming up.

Moonrise.

At last the long day's drudging journey was over. The horses had been tended to, sougans were unfolded and a rough meal had been prepared and laid out on the tailgate of the wagon. The head driver bowed his head and prayed:

'Dear Lord, thanks again for the vittles. Amen.'

Everybody began eating at once with just one bone-weary guard assigned look-out duties from a rock ledge, leaning on his carbine. He watched his companions enviously and paid no attention to keeping watch.

Why should he?

For one thing, nobody was supposed to know about the shipment. For another, they'd been working their way down out of the Tocsin hills ever since sun-up that morning without seeing a single sign of anything human – which was just as expected in this god-forsaken stretch of country. This was no man's land, too rough and remote even for a wild Indian.

So the sentry yawned – and accidentally dropped his carbine with a great clatter.

What happened next was something to see as nine guards and four drivers and hostlers leapt away from their improvised table to snatch up rifles and take up defensive positions all around the squat little square-sided wagon whose moon-washed blue cover concealed a king's ransom in dust.

It was some time before they realized it had been a false alarm. First they started in cursing as they emerged from their positions, but pretty soon their rancour turned to relief, then good humor. One man laughed and another cussed the sentry in a good-natured kind of way;

'Damned if I know why we're so jittery,' the head guard declared, settling down to his plate of hambone stew once more. 'Like, who'd dast take a crack at an outfit our size?

Nothin' smaller than the Dakota Militia, I'm thinking.'

There were murmurs and grunts of agreement that floated up faintly over rocks and thornbrush to reach the ledge a hundred feet above where a man lay spread-eagled beneath that blazing moon, staring down.

Reece Bannerman's guntipper, swarthy Chav Cody, was also smiling in the night.

He'd been posted there throughout the day, waiting to determine whether the word their spy in town was feeding them about the big shipment was fact or fiction.

Now he knew.

'How many riders with the wagon?'

'More 'n a dozen, Reece, mostly big tough mine guards.'

'Alert?'

'You can say that again. Looked to me like none of them geezers is gonna sleep until that wagonload is safe and sound under lock and key in Buffalo Horn.'

'Sounds just like Shannon reckoned it

would be,' Bannerman murmured. 'OK, go get some chow, pard. You did fine.'

Chav Cody headed for the fire, shoulders hunched against the wind. It was always cold this high up, even in midsummer when the plains and prairies were baking. Blazer and Houston, who'd been listening avidly to every word of the report, rolled their eyes excitedly at their leader, whose hair tossed in the wind like the mane of a wild mustang.

'So,' Blazer said at last, 'what do you say, boss?'

'Pretty good.' Bannerman folded arms across his brawny chest and grinned. 'Matter of fact, damned good. I gotta hand it to the kid. He was right about everything, right down to the number of guards, when they'd be taking the trail, the time, everything.'

Blazer went on grinning but not Houston.

'Don't you reckon it's time we talked about that flash bastard, Reece. I mean, now he's gone off leavin' us to do all the risky work, I mean.'

Reb Houston was a man who nursed a

grudge. Shannon had made him look really bad down in Buffalo Horn, and Bannerman had withdrawn him back up into this stone valley as a result. The fact that Bannerman had signed the man on solely as a scout and spy – Shannon wanted no part in the actual robbery – still didn't set well with the big bruiser either. Nor had Shannon's cool and distant manner endeared him to Blazer either, who chimed in now:

'Reb's right, boss. I mean to say, either a man's in a bunch or he ain't.'

'You telling me how to run this outfit, mister?'

'Hell no, Reece. It's just that–'

'I hired you pilgrims on account you're good with guns and greedy. Like me. When that young joker crossed our tracks, lookin' to earn a quick dollar, I quizzed him and found out he really knows the trails and had a good head on him, but that he ain't no road agent. So I hired him to sniff round where we couldn't, and neither of you can say he ain't done a solid gold job.'

Bearded Blazer and ox-shouldered Houston exchanged glances. Then Blazer just shrugged and chuckled again. He was thinking of a wagon full of gold. So was Reb Houston, but he still wasn't happy about Shannon. He was on the verge of taking it further when Bannerman spoke again.

'Better see to Chav's hoss before he cools off too fast, Reb.'

The big man grunted and slouched off, Bannerman's eyes following him. He turned back at Blazer.

'It's a risky business, questioning my say-so, Joe boy. You'd better get that across to your saddle pard afore he steps over the line. Get my drift?'

Tough Blazer nodded. He'd ridden with Bannerman longest of the three, knew him best. Bannerman was clever, gutsy, and a hard man to catch, as the law of five states could attest. But he also possessed a volcanic temper and had a zero tolerance for even the faintest hint of opposition.

'Sure, boss,' he grunted, going after

Houston and leaving Bannerman alone.

As he wanted to be.

The outlaw boss was far more excited than he showed, had suffered through six months of running from the law worse than anyone realized. Now he could smell the big one he felt like a king. The night was his mate, the future his for the taking.

A fortune in yellow gold is not a lifeless, inanimate thing. Rather it has a presence, a life-force all its own that will not be suppressed regardless of what efforts might be made to do so. It pulses with its own inner power, and certain men for whom gold is god are attuned to its mystic signals; they sense it, feel it, smell it. And sooner or later, by one means or another, they will surely find it.

So it was with the Tocsin shipment, which, although clothed in secrecy, was now known of by not just one, but two bands of desperadoes with gold-madness in their eyes, each as ruthless and murderously ambitious as the other.

While the man in Buffalo Horn who bore the brunt of full responsibility for the safety and security of this great treasure frittered the night away revelling with friends and family, seemingly preoccupied with nothing more important than scheming to break up an undesirable romance.

The dark gods would be laughing.

'More brandy, Mr Honeysett?'

'No thank you, daughter.'

'Mr Wylder?'

'Much obliged.'

Maureen signalled to the servant-girl who came quickly and silently to pour a little more French brandy into Wylder's balloon glass. The meal was over and the party had moved into the drawing-room. Milly Honeysett, who had always played the role of hostess since the mother's death, smiled at her father.

'More brandy, Father?'

'No, er – yes.' The banker tipped his glass

to his lips and drained it. He extended it, and the girl refilled it. As she moved away her father noticed the quick look she gave the tall man standing at his side. He smiled. Although unattractive himself, Buffalo Horn's premier citizen liked to be surrounded by stylish and interesting people.

Wylder, he felt, qualified on both counts. Indeed, he'd been quite taken by the town's impressive newcomer, and was flattered by the fellow's attention and company over what had otherwise been something of a tough week.

'Cheers,' he said, raising his glass. But he merely sipped as he subjected the other to a long, close scrutiny, scheming brain working overtime.

In his calculating way, he was sizing up Wylder's marriage potential. His daughters were approaching maturity. He was having trouble matching up the older girls, for as soon as any potential suitor clapped eyes on Della they were gone.

He sighed and scowled. That Della! Not

only would she not stop ruining her elder sisters' prospects, she now seemed to be forming an attachment to a totally unsuitable person.

Shannon.

He turned the name slowly over in his mind. What sort of handle was that anyway? His jowels sagged. Most likely an outlaw alias, if he was any judge.

'Not enjoying your own party, Rory?' Wylder interrupted his thoughts.

'Huh? Oh, forgive me, Nate.' He tapped his temple. 'Pressures of business, you understand?'

'I certainly do. Why, right at this moment, even with all your lovely daughters flitting around to distract me, I can't get my mind off that deal I discussed with you. You know? The one involving constructing a spur line for the S and B Line to circumvent the Chilton Badlands?'

'Ah, surely, surely. Knew you'd understand. But really, my dear fellow, shouldn't a fellow of your age be a little concerned that he should be burdened about business matters when there is so much beauty about?'

Wylder chuckled, man-to-man.

'Rory, glad you brought that up, for I think you must know that I'm greatly taken by your daughter–'

'Milly?' he broke in optimistically if unrealistically. He knew which daughter the man was interested in. He was no different from all the other Della admirers, except for the fact that he seemed to have more assurance, experience and rock-solid background than any of them. He sighed and shrugged. 'No, of course you mean ... oh yes, Mrs Darby?'

The glamorous widow had been ogling Wylder all night. 'I'm trying to convince your musicians it's time we began dancing, Rory pet,' she said, not taking her eyes off his companion. 'And I insist you be my partner for the first, Mr Wylder. Or may I call you Nate?'

Wylder clicked his heels and gave a little bow.

'My great pleasure, dear lady–' he began, but broke off as Della ran, not walked, straight by them, making for the doors. He heard the lift in the room noises and turned sharply to see the man Brazos standing beneath the lights.

He flicked a quick glance at Honeysett, who was scowling hard. The widow was no longer ogling Wylder, but was standing on tip-toes to see what all the fuss was about.

The banker imagined he heard the wretched female sigh: 'Ohh ... yummy!' And then she was gone, primping at her hair and practising her most welcoming smile.

The eyes of the two men met, Honeysett slack-jawed, Wylder's scowl hard as the core of a rifle barrel. The banker drew a long breath.

'All right, Nate, we both know the score. It's Della you like, and damn me if I might not be happy to say she might be all yours someday – providing you take full opportunity of this situation to help me force her into seeing the difference between a gentleman and a range bum. Or am I being too damned blunt for your taste?'

'Rory,' he smiled, 'we understand one another perfectly.'

It took some time for Della to escort the late arrival through the crowd, for everybody seemed interested in making the acquaintance of the young man who had the whole town talking, even if for some of the wrong reasons. Teenage girls and plump matrons appeared a little standoffish on first introduction, but a scowling Honeysett saw just how quickly they seemed to warm up when the damned saddle bum stopped to smile and chat – with Della hanging onto his arm as though cinched to him.

'No need to introduce you gentlemen,' Della said with a dazzling smile when at last they broke through. 'And will you please cheer up, Papa? You look as sore as an old daddy bear who's just lost all his honey.'

How unwittingly apt, Honeysett thought, then put on a big mine host smile for the benefit of those gathering around.

'Not glum at all, princess,' he assured. 'Matter of fact I was just laughing at a rather splendid story our friend Nate was recounting.' He turned to the tall man at his side who was looking at Shannon keenly. 'Rory, let's hear it again. All of us.'

Wylder obliged with his tale, yet somehow it didn't seem to impress anybody the way it had his host. It was amusing enough yet Wylder knew he hadn't delivered it well. As a consequence he felt unreasonably angry as Della, who was in stellar form tonight, related one of the many stories with which she had often entertained her admirers at Chinnick's.

Everybody laughed, which didn't improve Wylder's mood any. He just couldn't understand what was amiss. Normally he was at his very best on such occasions. He didn't realize that Honeysett's daughter had affected him more than he knew.

Either lust or love was throwing him off his stride. And added to this was the reality that Shannon was surprising him as much as he was Honeysett.

Wylder had already adjudged the man to be as dangerous and, likely, smart enough. But he'd not expected him to walk into this carefully laid trap and turn it into some sort of social triumph in the way he flattered and charmed all the women with an almost palpable charm, none of which had been in evidence previously.

And Rory wasn't helping: 'You're letting him take up the running!' the banker hissed in his ear. 'Do something, damnit!'

'Relax!' Wylder almost snapped, and wished he could take his own advice.

Della finally finished her tale to hearty laughter. Brandy-glasses were raised, maids bustled to and fro, chandelier-light glowed on rich tapestries and Brussels carpets and elegant furnishings.

Cassie then played a carefully rehearsed piece on the piano, before Milly sang for the company, after which the three-piece band was requested to play some kind of fiery Mexican dance.

Wylder was making for Della when the girl whispered something to Shannon, who immediately jumped up and demonstrated a fiery dance, twisting and stamping his heels so dynamically that Mama Chondo was drawn from her kitchen to clap her hands and shout '*Ole!*'

So it continued with Shannon plainly having the evening of his life while Wylder continued to find himself unable to grasp the social initiative, no matter how hard he tried.

And soon he was no longer trying, but growing angrier every minute. Ignoring the attentions of a cute plump young matron in jewels and silk, he watched Shannon and Della dancing together. Shannon didn't look like a gunfighter any longer; he simply looked like a handsome boy at a party. And Della, he thought irrationally, appeared indecently young – causing him to feel like an angry old man in his early thirties.

Until finally the dark side of Nate Wylder – the real and menacing underside –

surfaced and took over.

It was time for coffee and cakes as Wylder held a freshly lighted Honeysett Cuban cigar in his hand and approached the circle surrounding Della and Shannon.

'That's a fine shirt,' he complimented Shannon.

Shannon looked up warily. 'Thanks.'

'Silk, isn't it?'

'Uh, huh.'

'Imitation?'

'Real thing, I guess.'

Wylder appeared impressed. 'Real silk, eh? Must have set you back a few bucks?'

'Must have.'

The answer was a rebuff but Wylder seemed not to notice. He raised his voice so that it carried.

'Must be better money in drifting than there used to be,' he stated.

He glanced around. Things were going quiet and everyone was looking his way now, Shannon icily, Honeysett warningly. The banker was telling him this wasn't how it was supposed to go. Wylder ignored him. His veneer had slipped to reveal a hint of what lay beneath.

'I guess I must be in the wrong line of business,' he continued. 'It took me quite a few years hard and a lot of honest work before I could afford silk shirts. What say you, Rory?'

The banker looked unsettled. The room was very quiet by this time. As though sensing her young man's annoyance, Della reached out and rested her hand on Shannon's arm.

'Perhaps you could give me some pointers, boy?' Wylder insisted. 'You know? How to dress smart without wearing yourself out working.'

Suddenly people were talking in an attempt to defuse what appeared to be a budding scene. Honeysett was trying to catch the eye of the musicians as Shannon moved away from a concerned Della now to confront the taller man.

Wylder sneered. 'What's the matter,

sonny? Did I say the wrong thing, perhaps?'

'What is it, Wylder?' asked the whispering voice. 'Is it Della. She told me you were interested in her, but I figured she had to be joking.'

Wylder paled. 'What made you think that?'

'Where I hail from a feller looks around for somebody near his own age. Della's seventeen. If you're not double her age I'm no judge.'

Shannon's last words carried a sting in the tail.

'Where you hail from?' Wylder countered, breathing heavily through his mouth. 'That raises an interesting point, drifter. Why don't you tell us all where you do hail from. And while you're at it, what you do for a living. Della, I'm sure you'd like to know these things as well.'

'Please, Mr Wylder,' Della said sharply. 'We're having a lovely evening, and I'd thank you not to spoil it.'

'The hell with that!' Wylder almost

snarled, but Honeysett intervened.

'Now, that'll be quite enough, Nate.'

Wylder swung on him, all restraint gone now. 'You too, eh, Rory? You're siding with the saddle tramp who's feeling up your daughter behind your b–'

That was as far as it got. Moving like lightning, Shannon reached the man and crunched a short, vicious right to the jaw. Wylder's eyes rolled in their sockets and he would have hit the floor had not a houseboy grabbed him, lowering him to a chair.

Wylder was coming out of it, conscious of the shocked silence, of Shannon looming over him.

'You've had your say, now I'll have mine, Wylder. Sure, I'm a drifter, like you say. But I rate that higher than a businessman like you who travels round with a killer and a safe-breaker.'

Uproar.

The evening collapsed at that point. Struggling to his feet, Wylder attempted to defend himself, to explain. But Shannon had the ammunition: the recollection of a wanted dodger on Harry Brown, nee Burg, plus knowledge of the lethal record of gunslinger Conway Stack. So assured was he in contrast with a stunned and fumbling Wylder, that Honeysett, in an attempt to salvage what was left of his party, finally ordered his guest to leave.

Wylder left immediately. He went swiftly and without a word, the rage inside threatening to choke him. He stormed across the front veranda where Stack glanced up in surprise, crashed the heavy doors behind him then took giant strides down the flagged pathway to the *zaguán* gates where the nimble *pistolero* finally caught up.

'What the hell's goin' on, Nate?' Stack panted as they hurried on towards the lights of the nearest saloon.

'That bastard knows too much. Knows your record, knows Harry.'

'Who knows?'

'Shannon.' Wylder paused to catch his breath. He glared back at the house and said clearly, 'Get rid of him.'

The gunman's eyes widened. 'Kill him?'

'That's what I said.'

Stack grinned wolfishly. 'Sure thing, Nate. When?'

'Tonight.'

Drawing on his freshly lighted cigar, his eyes fixed straight ahead, Wylder strode on for the bright lights of Front Street. The lean killer, his own cigar cold between his fingers, stared after him.

CHAPTER 8

THE DUEL

Shannon stood towards the back of the bar, his hat tilted forward throwing his face into black shadow beneath the oil-lamps, swirling red wine in a glass held by the stem between thumb and forefinger.

Around him Chinnick's saloon bustled. Faro, chuck-a-luck, monte and roulette, all had their devotees in the Buffalo Horn's midnight hour. Percentage girls moved amongst the sports, flicking their hips and laughing with brittle voices, their tawdry brief outfits bright splashes of garish color against the uniform drab of ranch hands and working stiffs. One of these, a slender child-woman with a painted, pathetic face of half-witted lust, sidled up to the solitary Shannon. She smiled.

'Beat it,' he whispered.

She studied him insolently. She saw the smooth unlined cheeks, the sky blue eyes and the wide quirking mouth. She was swaying slightly on her heels. She was quite drunk.

'Hell!' she snorted. 'You the feller that's got 'em all walkin' on eggs? You ain't no older than me.'

He swung his head towards her, ready to retort. But he merely stared. She looked like a child, a lost, hopeless child. He said quietly, 'I can't buy you a drink. I'm waitin' for somebody.'

'You know, you look jus' like my brother, Billy. Sure, I know. Saloon gals ain't supposed to have families. But I got a brother and he looks just like you. He's a fine, good-lookin' boy.'

He stared over her head towards the batwings. He shoved his hand in his pocket and produced a wad of bills. He thrust them into her hand.

'Go buy yourself a new hat, honey.'

The girl stared at the money. 'But there's more than ten dollars here.'

'Make it a good hat. Now, will you shove off?'

Before he could react, she stood on her toes and kissed him on the mouth. Then she turned away, wending her uncertain way through the crowd. He made to wipe his lips then changed his mind, smiling crookedly. He raised his wine-glass again and sipped at it. The night had turned almost chill now with a faint mist drifting in front from the river.

A vaguely familiar voice sounded at his elbow.

'Whatever you just gave her made her night, Shannon.'

He turned to confront Taylock and Easy. It was the latter who'd spoken, the youthful attorney-at-law. Shannon nodded faintly.

'Mebbe so.'

'Reckoned you'd be at the Honeysetts' tonight,' Taylock chimed in.

'I was.'

'Oh, early night, huh?'

Shannon scowled. He didn't enjoy small talk at the best of times, and tonight was far from that. Easy had struck him as not a bad type – he'd had the guts to make some sort of a play outside Honeysett's home. But Taylock was too glib and patronizing, the sort of man who made him edgy.

'Early night,' he agreed flatly.

'You must be making headway in Buffalo Horn,' Taylock said. 'Socially, I mean. Not everybody gets invited to Honeysett's for supper, you know.'

Over the top of the batwings, Shannon saw a heavy-featured face briefly staring in. The face vanished instantly. Shannon felt his jaws tighten. Taylock was saying something about how they'd have to get together seeing as he was spending considerable time in their town.

'Don't suck up to me, man,' he said coldly. 'I don't like it.'

The man paled, his mouth hanging open foolishly. He seemed about to make an angry retort, but prudently changed his mind. Red-faced, he turned to Easy.

'Come on, Jim. That's all the thanks we get for trying to be friendly.'

Easy shot him a keen look, then sauntered off at Taylock's heels. Shannon watched them, his face expressionless. They belonged to a breed he didn't much care for, yet he took little pleasure in cutting them down.

But tonight anybody standing near him might just get shot.

This man had lived with the gun long enough to catch the whiff of cordite ahead of time. Hancock's brief appearance at the batwings only confirmed what he'd already sensed:

They were after him.

'Another wine, Mr Shannon?'

He turned to Old Bo. He'd grown to like the ancient horn-gray barkeep with the shrewd, warm eyes.

'No ... thanks,' he replied. He placed a dollar on the bar. 'But have one yourself.' He was spending money like a railroad tycoon – but then, money mightn't be of any use to him after tonight.

Old Bo thanked him without fawning and shuffled off to serve some thirsty ones. Shannon looked beyond the crowds, out past the batwings and windows where that unseasonal midnight mist was silently drifting by.

He looked down at his hands, working the slender fingers. A man knew what he could do. He was ready.

He slid his empty glass along the mahogany, hitched the shell belt around his middle and walked out of the saloon.

He stepped quickly aside from the doors, out of the light. He got his back against the painted clapboards. The streetlamps stood ghostly in the mist, their globes eerie blobs of light along Front.

There were few abroad now.

A towner clomped by on solid polished boots. He saw Shannon standing there in the shadows, nodded uncertainly and kept on. Two young cowboys, reeling a little, came from the saloon, clambered into the saddles of waiting horses and clattered off south. Even the cowboys here seemed tame and well-behaved, Shannon mused wryly.

There was no sign of the enemy, but he knew he was out there.

He thought about Stack, Brown and Hancock. He'd identified Brown on sight as a safebreaker wanted in Wyoming from some wanted dodgers that had stuck in his mind; a jittery little crook with soft clever hands. Hancock was tall, beefy-shouldered and battered – a bruiser and thug, if his guess was good, certainly no gunshark.

Which left Conway Stack.

Stack had gunshark stamped all over him. He'd realized that from the outset, for it was the look he likely had himself. The danger would have to be Stack. Well, a man couldn't have it easy all the time. Instinct told him that slender, hard-boned Stack might be the real McCoy. But he supposed he'd asked for it. He'd baited Wylder at the house and read murder in the man's eyes. He nodded. Sure, Wylder had slipped his *pistolero* off his leash. Men like Wylder didn't let anybody get away with what he'd said and done tonight.

Something stirred in shadows across the street.

Shannon froze, his right hand instinctively wrapping around his gunbutt. The movement was located in an alley-mouth, vague and dim. He waited with the patience of a hostile. Two men emerged from the saloon opposite, Taylock and Easy. They stood for a moment, talking. Then Taylock spotted him against the saloon wall.

'What's going on, Shannon?' the man called curiously.

'Get the hell away from here!' Shannon snarled, eyes cutting back to the alley-mouth.

'Now see here!' Taylock, replied hotly.

'There's going to be gunplay,' Shannon whispered hoarsely. 'So get the Sam Hill out of here before you walk into some stray lead.'

The young men traded startled glances, then hurried swiftly away along the walk. The movement in the alley-mouth had ceased with their appearance. It recommenced now. The shape there became clear. It was a man. Another handful of seconds and he could identify the bulky outline of Hancock.

The big man came to a halt on the walk, staring directly across the street at him. Shannon felt the chill of the fog on his face and hands. Hancock remained unmoving, a misshapen statue. Had he made one move towards his hip, Shannon would have gunned him down. Instead he kept his hands in his pockets. After a minute, he simply turned and moved off.

Hancock was acting as look-out for the gunman, Shannon knew. He knew Stack had to be close by. Real close, was his guess. Well, he'd let the man come to him. He had a wall at his back and he was in shadow – as good a defensive situation as a man could hope to find on short notice.

Conway Stack appeared suddenly five minutes later, materializing piece by piece through the fog tendrils, lean, silent and dangerous. 'Shannon!'

'Yeah?'

The gunman halted some seventy feet distant, leaning forward. 'I got something for you, Shannon!'

Shannon's eyes raked the street beyond the man. No sign of Hancock now. There was just him and Stack. He felt the sure cold knot of hardness behind his belt-buckle and knew he was ready. He might have lost count of the times he'd had that sensation, but a man never lost count of those he'd killed.

'You want what I've got, Shannon?'

Shannon pushed off the wall and went cat-footed across the porch, pausing at the steps.

His adversary stood with boots wide-planted, Prince Albert coat flicked back to reveal the mute challenge of gun and shell belt. The man's hands hung loosely at his sides. Confident, Shannon assessed. Real confident.

Shannon descended the steps. Had he glanced behind he would have seen the windows of Chinnick's filled with staring faces. He didn't look. He was focused on his man to the exclusion of all else.

A dog sounded somewhere along the street, the sound clear and loud in the hush. Shannon settled his weight lightly on the balls of his feet. He didn't speak. He was to fight, not jaw.

'Think you are somethin', eh, Shannon?'

No response.

'Hot with a gun as you are with your

flappin' mouth?'

Silence.

Now Stack's hard face twitched and he was sliding into his draw, all blinding speed and gun rage.

Yet his adversary whispered to himself: 'Way too slow!' as his .45 leapt out of leather like a live thing and the murderous crash of gunfire rocked the street to engulf the other man, whose weapon was still only half-way clear of the leather.

The mortally hit gunfighter staggered backwards on rubber legs until the backs of his knees caught the leading edge of the gallery of Bilby's store. He stood swaying, still struggling to get his gun up. From the center of the street, Shannon fired again. Stack fell on his back.

Fingering fresh shells into his smoking gun, Shannon slowly crossed the street, the reverberations of the gunshots still batting to and fro between the false-fronts. There was no need to hurry. He felt nothing, only gratitude that he was alive. He'd never killed a man who hadn't tried to kill him first. This one had tried, and he'd like to know why.

Conway Stack was staring straight up at him from the dirt, wild-eyed, choking on blood. 'All that gold...' he gasped over and over. 'All that gold ... all that gold...'

His voice cut off as though a hand had clapped over his mouth. Shannon dropped to one knee and placed a hand over his heart. Wylder's hard-case was dead.

He rose and finished reloading his gun. They were spilling out of Chinnick's and the Red Horse now, swarming about him, clustering by the still figure in front of Bilby's darkened store. He stood remote from all the hysteria. He was thinking of what Stack had said about the gold. Could it be the gold? And if Stack knew, how could Wylder not know...?

Sheriff Bean interrupted his thoughts, pushing his way through the mob, rubbing sleepy eyes.

'Well, what happened here, Shannon?'

'He called me out.'

'That's so, Sheriff,' Jim Easy weighed in. 'Me and Jack saw the whole thing from yonder doorway. He forced Shannon to draw. It was self-defence.'

The lawman's shoulders slumped. What was happening to his solid, law-abiding town these days?

'Come see me in the mornin' and we'll get the details,' he muttered wearily, and made his bow-legged way to the store to examine the body with gaping holes in its chest. Shannon turned away. Chicken Pickles, the lamplighter, clapped him on the back, congratulating him. He slapped the man's hand away with such violence that he stumbled and fell.

'It's not some kind of game, stumblebum!' he hissed. And next moment heard himself whisper, 'All that gold...'

He sighted big Matt Hancock on the fringe of the crowd now, pale and shocked-looking. But when Wylder, Brown-Berg came hurrying into view, he stepped backwards in the throng and moments later was making his way down a darkened alley.

He went directly to the Federation Hotel where the Wylder party was staying. The desk was deserted, the lobby empty – everyone had gone off to rubberneck on Front. He spun the register and found Wylder's suite number. He took the stairs three at a time, then went out onto the first-floor balcony to make his way along to the french doors giving onto the presidential suite.

Hunkering down in the darkness, he waited.

An hour later before the Wylder party entered the suite with a great clatter. Through the glass, Shannon saw the tall man hurl his hat into one corner and his opera-cloak and cane into another. He didn't have to strain any to hear the angry discussion on Stack's death. Then the voices dropped some and he pricked his ears to hear what he'd come for. They were now calmly discussing the Tocsin shipment and their plans to take it, plans which Wylder said quite clearly would go ahead regardless of tonight's drama. They had the combination – the rest would be easy. They didn't need Stack.

Shannon didn't wait for more. He'd heard enough. He went over the balcony railing, slid down a stanchion and dropped into the yard to make his way directly for the livery. As he walked, he planned. The liveryman was peeved at being disturbed, the gelding far crankier. Shannon ignored them both, rode quietly out of town and headed west for the Sawteeth.

CHAPTER 9

BADMEN'S ADIOS

The dawn hour was chill in the high valley and a fine mist moved sluggishly between crumbling battlements, twisting sinuously around the awesome, brooding silhouettes of ancient Indian stone gods.

Chav Cody was perched upon the look-out rock. Bannerman, as befitted the leader, hunkered down by the fire and fashioned a cigarette while Houston handed the horses grain-feed from a sack in a lower cave. Blazer was off someplace with his gun, looking for a rabbit for the pot.

Heads jerked up at the sound of hoof striking rock. Cody, seated with his rifle resting across his thighs, jumped up and squinted into the grayness.

'Who goes?' he called.

'Shannon!'

'And about freakin' time,' growled Bannerman, bouncing erect on thick muscular legs.

Cody lowered his rifle as he recognized the lean shape of the rider, the big ugly horse. Shannon passed below his look-out position with a barely perceptible nod. When he reached the stone slabs below the caves, Bannerman, Houston and Blazer were grouped together by the fire, expectant and impatient. Cody clambered down to join them, with his rifle angled at the ground.

Bannerman slapped his barrel chest and knotted powerful features in a scow.

'You were expected last night, boy.'

Shannon swung down silkily and passed the roan's lines to Houston.

'He needs some oats, Reb.'

Houston made to object, but bit his brutal underlip. He was afraid of Brazos now. He took the lines and stomped away, the horse following with a display of bad grace. Shannon extended his hands to the licking flames and eventually glanced at Reece Bannerman.

'I got delayed last night.'

Bannerman made an O with his lips. 'And would that have been business or pleasure, mister?'

'Depends on your point of view, I guess.'

Shannon stared at the fire, rubbing his hands. Bannerman waited for him to elaborate but after a minute it grew plain that he'd said all he intended for the present. Bannerman nodded to Blazer.

'Better fix the man some joe, Joe.'

Blazer glared belligerently. 'Oh sure, Blazer do this, Cody come here, Houston tend the horses… Seems everybody here has to pull his weight in this outfit except bright boy here. He's been gone more'n twenty-four hours, moseys in like a goddamn lord, tells us next to nothin', and you want me to fetch coffee for him. Well, I can tell you that–'

'Coffee!' Bannerman rapped. 'And hobble your lip.'

For a moment it seemed Blazer might rebel. He glared at Bannerman heatedly, then at Shannon, who met his glare unblinkingly across the fire. It was Blazer's gaze that dropped first. Kicking at the fire, he flung away.

Bannerman locked his hands behind his back and rocked on his heels. Cody, short stocky legs planted solidly upon the rock, the rifle held across his hips, said quietly:

'The man is right, Reece. We're gettin' mortal sick of Shannon livin' high on the hog in town and then showin' up late and empty-handed.'

Bannerman's heroically ugly head bobbed.

'You hear that, boy? You might as well know I feel likewise. Now, I signed you on as a look-out for us in town on account of you and Reb are the only ones in the bunch without their mugs pasted on truebills all over the Dakotas. When you contended Reb looked like foulin' things up in there, I let you take over the job of finding us a target, someplace we could knock over quick and get our hands on some easy ready. Now, I ain't saying you didn't do real good – at first. You told us about that gold shipment you got wind of, and then about Nate Wylder and his crew showing up suspiciously right about the same time. Top work, no doubtin' it. But, hell and damnation, there's been precious little since, I reckon you'd agree?'

'Maybe.'

'Maybe? Listen, son, the gold is due tomorrow afternoon and we're fixing to go after it Saturday night when the mine guards have gone home and there's only bank nightwatchmen left. But we've been waiting for you to come up with some workin' ideas on how best to go about it. Well, do you have those ideas, boy? You've had plenty time to come up with them, I'm thinking.'

Bannerman's tone still held a certain outdoor amiability, but the face behind the words was hard-edged and aggressive now. He was bracing Shannon and everybody knew it.

'Reece,' Shannon said quietly. 'I want to quit.'

Bannerman's eyes flared white-hot.

'You drunk, boy? Nobody quits Reece Bannerman.'

'So they say. But it's only been two weeks since I just moseyed into your camp lookin' for a job. So far I'm not in too deep, and that's where I'd like to leave it. Not in too deep. I reckon I could pull out now without lettin' you down any.'

'Know why I hired you that day, son? You had the right look, and I needed a good scout in town. You were eager enough to ride for me then.'

'That was then.'

'So, what's different now?'

Shannon stared into the fire. He was just a fast-gun drifter who had never held down a regular job. But there was always a quick dollar to be made anyplace if you weren't fussy about what you did. Chance had brought him into the gang's orbit, and he'd proved his skills in scenting out word of the gold shipment, and would likely have gone on to play his part in the planned robbery had not something happened that he'd never encountered in his solitary life before.

'You aim to talk or day-dream, boy?' Bannerman demanded after a silence.

'Let's you and me talk alone, Reece.'

The corners of Bannerman's mouth hooked downwards. 'After our joe, mebbe. But I can tell you now, you ain't quittin'.'

'Mebbe I could buy my way out?'

Bannerman fixed him with a long cold look. This rugged hellion was a different proposition from Wylder. Whenever possible, Wylder hired men to be brave for him. Bannerman never needed to do that.

He slapped his gun butt. 'The only ticket out of my mob is stamped .45.'

Shannon didn't even blink. He'd ridden double with death behind him all his young life. He knew he could beat Bannerman, but not all of them. He could die here – for death had surely been waiting to grab him up ever since he'd blasted the first brute who'd tried to kill him as a kid, and he'd been facing up to that same breed ever since.

He built a brown-paper cigarette, lighted up and spun the dead match into the fire. And a pang, like an icy wind blowing from across the frozen plains of death passed over his heart and shivered it like a leaf. It was as though the men he'd killed were all suddenly whispering to him on that mist-wind. This had never happened before, but then, he'd never really cared a damn for anyone before. Della Honeysett had walked into his life and suddenly he didn't want to hire his skills or his gun to men like Reece Bannerman any more. It was as simple or as complicated as that.

Bannerman flung his coffee dregs into the flames and scratched his belly as he studied Shannon. Reb Houston's red-rimmed eyes were also upon him, as was Cody's dark gaze. Joe Blazer's bitter stare drilled at him from the shadows, waiting, likely hating him because he was little more than a kid yet seemed to possess a kind of lethal authority that scared a man.

'You are not saying anything…'

'Alone, Reece.'

'We're all pals here.'

'We talk alone or not at all.'

There was a sucked intake of breath all round. Shannon's whispery voice cut, his eyes were chips of blued steel. Now he was bracing Bannerman. And nobody did that. Ever.

Yet after a hanging moment in which the faint whiff of gunsmoke seemed to mingle with the ghostly mist, Bannerman shrugged off his anger, ran fingers through his thatch and reached a decision.

'Back off, boys. Go find something to do.'

Sullen and resentful, the outlaws did as ordered. The outlaw's thick brows hooked upwards like quivering question marks.

'So … let me guess, bucko. The girl? The one you and Reb tangled over who he says you've been buggy-riding around ever since, while you were supposed to be digging up my information?'

'Could be.'

'I said – is it the girl?'

Shannon nodded. 'Yeah.'

Bannerman studied at his boots. They were in need of a good rub-up with ham-fat. He spoke quietly.

'You're putting me on a spot, young Shannon. If I let one man quit, hell, next time things get rough everybody's headin' for the door. Any good reason I should let you go and not anybody else?'

'I've got information that should be worth

a trade.'

'You've been holdin' out on me?'

'You want to hear it or not?'

'It had better be good.'

'If it meant the difference between your gettin' hands on that gold or missin' out, would that be good enough?'

'I mean to get it anyways.'

'You could go down ... unless you know what I can tell you.'

'What's to know? You already tipped me there'll just be four bank guards there over the weekend. We show up midnight Saturday with the dynamite and–'

'You'd need enough dynamite to blow away half the town to even mark that safe. In any case, the gold wouldn't still be there for you to grab if you tried.'

'Not there?' Bannerman said hollowly. His face paled, the ugliness exaggerated. Without haste, he took out his big black-barrelled Peacemaker with the bluing worn off the barrel. He let the gun hang at his side without looking at it. Fifty yards distant,

Cody, Houston and Blazer took their cue and also took out their cutters. Shannon again felt old Death's hoary breath, yet appeared the most relaxed man in the valley of stone.

'Boy,' Bannerman breathed, 'I get the real bad feeling you've been holding out on me. That's bad. That's mighty bad...'

'I just found out what I know tonight, and by chance. But I reckon it's my ticket to ride. You willin' to deal?'

'Deal? Sounds more like you're black-mailin' me, Sonny Jim.'

'This can mean a hundred thousand to you, Reece. An easy hundred thousand if you play it smart.'

A long spine-tingling moment. Then: 'Deal then, damn you. But only if you got the goods.'

'Stack's dead. Wylder sicced him onto me and I shot him down.'

Bannerman's eyes widened. 'Stack was a class gun. Big rep.'

'All hat and no cattle as it turned out.'

'This ain't enough to buy your ticket, mister.'

'You recall how we pondered if that bunch maybe had eyes on the gold too? Well, now we know. Wylder means to empty that safe Saturday night himself. And he can do it.'

'The hell you say! How–?'

'That sidekick of his they call Brown. He's Harry Berg – Cracker Berg they call him in Cheyenne. I tabbed him from the start from the wanted dodgers I'm always checkin' out just in case I'm on one.'

'So, you knew this and didn't tell me?'

'Don't sweat. You're hearing about it now. All of it. I heard Wylder plannin' to hit the bank at midnight. Seems to me if you showed up nice and quiet, waited for Berg to produce his box of tricks – let them do all the hard work – you and the boys could just jump them and ride away rich. How does that sound?'

Bannerman's eyes hadn't left Shannon's in minutes.

'Sounds like the best information anybody's ever given me, son. If it's true, that is.'

'I don't lie.'

The other barely heard. Bannerman's head was spinning. He'd gone gold-loco the moment he'd first learned of the Tocsin shipment several days earlier, had immediately sat down to figure how to get his hands on it. The plan of action he devised was pure Bannerman: take out the guards, dynamite the vault, blast anyone who tried to stop them. As subtle as a snowslide, but that was how he worked, and often enough succeeded.

Now he was looking at a whole new scenario and needed time to get his head around it.

But Shannon was seeing the sun breaking through the mist.

'Well, what do you say?'

Bannerman was gold-blinded and therefore might have been ready to kiss the devil to succeed any which way he might. His conciliatory mood wouldn't last, but for the moment it was all-important.

'OK, Shannon, you're free.'

Shannon suppressed a grin.

'See you, Reece.' He turned and headed for the caves to collect his roll and kit.

'Just one thing, boy,' Bannerman called after him. 'I'm mainly letting you ride because I figure you can keep your mouth shut. I'd take it personal if you was to let anything slip about me and the boys, now or ever.'

Shannon just nodded. He wanted out of here fast. Maybe he half-trusted Bannerman. But not the others, who watched him like hawks as he went by.

He climbed up to his cave and fashioned a neat warbag comprising slicker, ground-sheet and sougan. He slung it over his shoulder and clambered down again for his mount. Cody, Houston and Blazer now stood in a circle around the fire with Bannerman, the early sun in their watching eyes. He loaded up the roan which tried to savage him, clipped it beneath the jaw with his elbow, swung up.

Four hard faces met him as he approached the fire. He could see Bannerman had already told them. He'd achieved and maintained some kind of rapport with the outlaw boss himself, but there was no love lost between himself and the others. He was too young and arrogant for such as they, even if he did excel at his work. But now he'd quit they just might decide to settle some grudges.

Better not, his cold gaze warned. With the advantage of horseback and with the men bunched tight together as they were, he knew he could kill two, maybe even three before they got him. He hoped they wouldn't try. That they'd have brains enough to figure that a burst of gunplay could easily cost them both life and a king's ransom. He singled out only Bannerman as he rode by.

'So long, Reece.'

'See you when the grapes get ripe, Shannon.'

Now they were in back of him as the

gelding picked its way through ancient rock rubble. Ten feet, twenty, thirty ... the muscles of his back coiled like a clenched fist as though in anticipation of a bullet.

His ears strained for the first sound of steel hissing from stiff leather, the scuff of boot leather against rock, the sharp intake of breath – any indicators of treachery that would have brought him whipping about with a raging sixshooter in his fist.

Another hundred feet and he was out of easy range. The sun struck him fully as he rode into the open and his shadow leapt far across the valley floor, a stick man on a horse with legs a hundred feet long.

He allowed the roan to cover a good distance further before hipping round in the saddle. The quartet was still visible, still staring after him. Bannerman had kept his word. He might be a butchering bastard, yet he Shannon now half-hoped he might end up with the gold. Better he than Wylder. At least Bannerman was a man, not a smooth-lying yellow dog like the other.

He felt curiously detached as the long horse-miles carried him towards the distant plains. He'd now severed himself from the grab for the gold. It all seemed petty and unimportant now there was so much else in his life that was immeasurably more exciting and worthwhile. He was thinking of that something as the big horse picked its surly way along the faint trace of the trail. Away to the south, the day's first buzzard took to the sky.

CHAPTER 10

TO THE VICTOR

Brazos picked up a smooth white pebble between his fingers and flicked it at the water. It landed with a small popping sound, sending smooth circles rippling across the sky-blue surface of the wide rock pool.

Grazing nearby on the end of a lead rope beneath the protection of a ponderosa pine, the roan looked up with a sharp eye and glared reproachfully.

The man gathered up another pebble and pinged it at the horse. It found horsehide, but the big saddler merely swung its rump disdainfully. It wasn't accustomed to its owner in this frivolous mood. Shannon just grinned and stretched his arms luxuriously. A man could grow lazy awful quick just lying around in the sun and taking the occasional dip, he told himself, especially at a place as pretty and remote as Spirit Spring.

This was where Della had taken him following his dust-up with Houston at Chinnick's saloon.

It was a favored picnicking spot for the Honeysetts and many others from Buffalo Horn, an idyllic tree-shadowed refuge in cool foothills just far enough from Front Street to give the feeling that you could be lost in the wilderness.

Shannon had made his way here the

previous day following his showdown with Bannerman. It was now late Saturday afternoon. He'd visited the town last night, meeting with Della by pre-arrangement, discussing many things including the gunfight which he now hoped might prove to be his last. Ever.

He hadn't been within miles of the town today nor did he intend going in. The shipment had arrived on schedule and was now 'securely' locked away in Honeysett's fine new safe with bank guards mounting a round-the-clock watch.

His information-gathering chore for Bannerman was completed.

Now, if he played no further role in whatever came about, he reckoned he could convince himself he'd had no involvement in whatever might happen from here on in. Self-deception and selective memory had always been vital tools in his survival techniques throughout the solitary and often violent existence he'd always known, a life now hopefully drawing to an end.

His conscience would not trouble him. It had been dormant ever since his first kill. Maybe now everything was changing for him he might dare to release it again, breathe fresh life into it.

Be like other men.

Around sundown he prodded his little fire into fresh life and dropped bacon and flapjacks into the skillet, set a pot of coffee to burble away in the coals.

He groomed the gelding while the meal cooked, fed it red-corn nubbins out of his hand. Each time the animal attempted to nip him he flicked its nose with his finger. It was an old game. No matter how much the horse enjoyed a delicacy, it still tried to bite.

He ate his solitary meal by firelight with the stars a tangled net of fire stretched across a vast black sky. He'd never felt so at peace. He cleaned the utensils, rubbing them clean in yellow spring sand before packing them neatly away in his possibles sack.

Leaning back against a tree with a freshly lit cigarette he concentrated on tomorrow –

and the tomorrows after that.

It all seemed crystal clear.

They would leave Bright's County, he and Della. He'd killed a man here, had come here with outlaws. They'd go someplace far off where he would live simply like other men, with her and because of her, never again to walk the wild side of the street.

He sat thus for several hours, watching the moon climb out of the badlands beyond the Sawteeth, relaxed and easy – until his iron will let him down and allowed harsh reality to intrude.

Suddenly he found himself unable not to dwell on what could be taking place in Buffalo Horn, where not one but two packs of desperadoes were primed and ready to go after Honeysett's yellow gold.

His jaws clamped hard.

Let them thrash it out how they would, he told himself angrily. Let them squabble, fight, most likely kill themselves over four black-handled crates of gold dust. Nothing to do with him now. He'd washed his hands of it all – like Pilate.

He was astonished to find himself unable to clear his conscience, as he'd always been able to do at will. Instead of sleeping, he prowled the night with one cigarette after another, kicking obstacles from his path. Eventually he turned in but lay restless in his bedroll until well after midnight, the scheduled time of Wylder's robbery attempt.

He lay on his back, struck by the contrast between the calm beauty of the night and images of whatever Wylder, Bannerman and God alone how many other bit players and sidekicks might be involved in right now at the Honeysett Banking Company.

And speculated; if there had been no Della he might have well been drawn in to tonight's events. Might even have been forced to kill somebody in cold blood – for the first time in his life. Then there could have been no turning back for him, no redemption.

He tried to find reassurance in this line of thinking. It didn't work. Yet somehow, despite

his strange mood, he dimly recalled con-
sulting his scrolled-steel fob-watch at around
1.30, and next he knew it was dawn. He'd
slept five hours!

He wasted no time. No breakfast, just
coffee black and hot and a waking cigarette
followed by a quick shave and he was ready
for the trail.

He was anxious to get back now. Today
would be the worst day, while the town was
recovering from its shock. But each day
after would be better than the one before.

He only hoped it had not been too bloody.
And foolishly tried to convince himself that
maybe there had been no bloodshed at all.

The sun came up when he was half-way to
town. He rode across the limestone regions
they'd crossed that first day, coming from
Buffalo Horn and making for the springs.

No Sabbath bells pealed across the
countryside calling the faithful to worship
today. But nobody was resting. He could see
the frenzy of activity on the streets as soon as
he topped out the last rise to bring the town

into clear view. People dashing this way and that, knots of excited citizens clustered all along wide Front Street, a pervading atmosphere of stress bordering on hysteria.

Well, what had he expected?

He entered the main stem looking relaxed in his saddle, but in the shadow of his hat his eyes were darting everywhere, missing nothing.

Agitated men and women returned his look, if not with suspicion then certainly with some uncertainty. For he was still regarded as a stranger here, and today, with their orderly world thrown in chaos, the people of Buffalo Horn were drawing together for strength and comfort – strangers not welcome.

Shannon just rode on by with the corners of his mouth quirking. It didn't matter a damn what they might think about him anyway. If you'd never belonged anyplace, no place could hurt you.

The center of activity was plainly the street outside the bank. Riding up, he soon spotted Taylock and McCoy with the mayor and a dozen others he knew by sight amongst the sea of faces. He might have been amused by the comic-opera shock stamping most faces had it been less serious. He felt secure in the cocoon of his detachment, but it was a feeling that wasn't destined to survive the first half-minute.

'What's goin' on here?' he demanded as he reined in.

They turned on him, surprised, dazed-looking.

'Don't you know? The bank's been robbed!' Buck Poley said loudly. 'We thought you…'

Poley cut himself off abruptly in mid-sentence. Shannon smiled grimly. They were so easy to read. Poley had been about to hint that he might have been involved. He didn't blame them for being suspicious; they had more reason than they knew.

He was expressionless again as he said, 'Much taken?'

'The shipment!' somebody shouted. 'A load of gold come in while you were away, and the bastards stole every last speck of it!'

'Shot and killed two of the guards,' another man supplied, grim-faced. 'Wallace and Corkill.'

Shannon's scalp pulled tight. That was the bark with the bite in it. Two men dead. He'd been loco to think it might have gone off without bloodshed. Now his conscience was at him like an aching tooth.

'Anythin' I can do?' he offered, and meant it.

For the first time, Rory Honeysett, whom he'd sighted up on the steps, pale as parchment, spoke up.

'You've already done enough, you ... you drifter!'

Shannon scowled.

'What do you mean, man? I didn't have anythin' to do with you losin' your money.'

'I'm talking about my daughter, as well you know, gunman or whatever you call yourself. You wangled and sweet-talked your way into her affections, and now she's gone too.'

Front Street seemed to pitch and sway in Shannon's vision for a moment. Aware of a fierce constriction in his throat, he sprang down and thrust his way through the mob to the banker's side.

'Are you sayin' Della's missin'?'

'Della and my dust. Both gone!'

He shook his head. Nobody was making sense.

'Will someone tell me just what the hell happened?'

It was Jack Taylock who responded.

'From what the two surviving guards told us, we've been able to piece most of it together, Shannon. Around midnight those four men were just sitting around inside the bank, and next thing anyone knew there were three masked men busting in, armed to the teeth. They bailed up the guards then broke the lock on the screen doors leading down to the vaults. Then they went right up to the safe and … and opened it – knew the combination!'

'My wonderful safe!' the banker lamented. 'How could anyone have known the combination?'

'What about Della?' Shannon demanded.

'Well, after they'd opened the safe, the bandits forced the guards to tote the crates upstairs then load it aboard a wagon they had parked in the side lane. They were just about through when Wallace and Corkill busted loose and tried to jump them, brave lads.'

'Damn nigh succeeded too,' Gul McCoy supplied. 'But Wylder gunned them down.'

'Wylder? You sure?'

'Yeah, it was him all right. The guards half-guessed it could have been him from the start, but Bob Corkill ripped his bandanna off before he got bored and put it beyond doubt.'

'What happened to Della?' Shannon demanded, trying not to shout.

'Wylder abducted her,' Honeysett replied in a dead voice. 'I heard the shooting from the bank and rushed up the street, of course. Apparently Wylder had it all planned as his gang invaded my house as soon as I'd left. The girls were all up, of course, wondering what all the hullabaloo was about. He forced Della to dress at gunpoint and go with him.'

'Didn't she put up a fight?'

'He held a pistol at my mother's head,' Honeysett said. 'She had no choice.'

Shannon was still stunned, yet everything began to fall into place with terrifying clarity. Wylder must have been obsessed by Della, just like himself, but had ruined any chances he might have had with her at the house the night of the party. What he should have realized was that a man like that wouldn't just accept such a defeat and let it lie. Wylder had shown the breed he was by sending Stack to kill him.

Now he'd either abducted Della to square accounts with her, or to utilize her as a hostage should he need one. But the reasons didn't signify. All that mattered was that she was gone.

He shook his head and fought for control. He couldn't afford rage. He must think clearly. Now more than ever before.

'Why aren't all of you off runnin' Wylder

to ground?' he wanted to know.

'How could we?' Buck Poley complained. 'It was the middle of the night. We don't even know what route they took.'

'So, you did nothin'?'

The banker looked defensive. 'They're murderers, mad dogs. They showed that. What good would it be for more men to go after them and get killed?'

'It just might have got your daughter back, Honeysett. There were only three of them, goddamnit!'

'Three bloodthirsty killers,' Honeysett corrected. 'That mightn't mean much to a man like you who is so adept at killing–'

'Shut!' Shannon hissed. This was no time for wrangling. 'Tell me. Was anybody else seen about town last night, anyone suspicious?'

He was thinking about Bannerman as heads shook negatively, and both McCoy and Taylock replied, 'No,' watching him curiously, plainly wondering what he was driving at.

The way he was figuring – all the gunplay and uproar at the bank followed by the abduction at the Honeysett house would surely have forced Bannerman to change his original plan to jump the thieves as they quit the bank with the gold.

It figured that Bannerman's only alternative had been to wait and jump Wylder as he quit town.

He felt a chill at this thought, for Della was with Wylder now. Maybe at this very minute, Bannerman and Wylder could be fighting to the death over the spoils with Della caught up in the middle of it.

'Where's the sheriff?' he demanded.

'Oh, he took some of the boys and went off huntin' the robbers at first light,' somebody supplied.

'Why the hell didn't someone tell me that?'

'How's it concern you, Shannon?' a man wanted to know.

'Because I'm goin' after him to back his play,' he snapped. 'How many's the sheriff got with him?'

'Three,' declared Poley. 'Jim Easy and two cowboys.'

Shannon grimaced. 'Three volunteers out of a whole town!' he said bitterly, hating them all, contemptuous of every man of them who hadn't gone. And the most culpable of all, fat, righteous Rory Honeysett had stood back and allowed other men to risk their lives searching for his own daughter while he stayed behind griping about his gold.

All refused to meet his eye now. They were ashamed; his contempt was palpable.

He ran to his horse and vaulted into the saddle, causing the roan to rear and snort.

'Which way did Bean take?'

'North-west route they call the Badlands Trail,' supplied Poley.

He turned the fractious horse hard and fought to steady it. All eyes were upon him. His face was intent, tautly drawn. He leaned forward, hands tight on the reins, heels drawn out ready to kick the straining gelding into a gallop. He appeared more controlled yet somehow more dangerous than they'd seen him before. His very look inspired confidence and a touch of fear. Rory Honeysett rushed forward to seize his stirrup iron before he could go careening away.

'Shannon. Please find my gold. I'm responsible for it. I'll be ruined. I'll pay you handsomely, I swear. Promise you'll do your best.'

'And your daughter?'

The man flushed red. 'Of course ... I meant her as well.'

'But you didn't say so, did you, fat man?' He kicked his foot free and drove heels into horsehide, the banker stumbling and falling to the ground as he stormed away.

Shannon didn't look back.

He galloped the horse to the first corner, then cut down a side street leading to the north side of town. His rage against the towners was already fading as he concentrated on the trail ahead.

Every instinct told him this was the route to take. As part of his job for Bannerman, he'd circled Buffalo Horn several times searching for the best escape-route for the gang to take following the hold-up, and had recommended the north trail. It was the logical run-out route from the town – and he was guessing Wylder would also identify it as such. This trail was far from the Ranger outposts and eventually led through a remote section of badlands and on up into the Indian Territory beyond Rogue River, long a refuge for badmen of both Dakotas.

So – Wylder had fled north with Bannerman tailing him. He was no longer speculating; he was dead sure of it now.

He leaned low over his horse's neck and the town fell away behind.

There was any amount of fresh sign on the trail, but it wasn't difficult to pick up the prints of the sheriff and his party. A heavy overnight mist had sheened all earlier sign. Amongst the fresher tracks overlaying the old were the clear wheelmarks of a vehicle –

possibly a brougham toting a heavy load – judging by the depth of the depressions.

A heavy load. Like maybe four crates of gold, and a hostage?

He put several swift miles behind him before sighting four horsemen up ahead, coming his way. He kept the roan on at a gallop, not dragging it to a sliding halt until he was abreast of the group. Sheriff Bean stared at him with pain-hollowed eyes, his right arm hanging bloodied and useless at his side. Shannon realized Jim Easy was swaying in the saddle and clutching at his belly. The two unscathed cowboys stared at him, wide-eyed and scared-looking.

'You caught up with the bandits?' he guessed.

Bean shook his grizzled head. 'Reckon not.'

'But you're shot up…'

'Weren't Wylder.' Bean clamped his jaws grimly. 'It was four other hard cases I reckon were trailing the bank robbers from the brush. Three strangers and that bastard,

Houston. They opened up on us on sight, took us by surprise. Easy's shot up bad and I can't hold a gun. We had to turn back.'

'Guess they must have been part of hold-up gang we didn't know about,' the first cowboy speculated.

Shannon made no response, yet was certain he could figure what had happened. Bannerman had dogged Wylder from town, waiting for the right place to jump him. But the sheriff's bunch had overtaken them before they could strike and they'd turned on them. The posse had been chewed up, but was still lucky to have survived.

'What are you doing out here anyway?' the sheriff wanted to know, his face gray with pain.

'I'm goin' after them.'

'There's got to be seven or eight of them altogether. They'll butcher you.'

'They might try.'

He spurred away hard, hammering over a cottonwood saddle to hit a mile-long flat where arroyos scarred the landscape deeply to either side. Rocking in the saddle, he cleared his .45 and checked the action. Next he hauled his rifle from its scabbard. It was loaded and ready. He shoved it away and slapped the roan's neck. This was where the animal excelled. It was ugly and evil-tempered yet could run as long as a man could sit the saddle. The miles flowed swiftly beneath them, the sun climbing the sky. Then, dimly above the drumbeat of hoofs, Shannon heard the sound of guns.

'Comfortable, my dear?'

'What do you think?'

Wylder just shrugged. 'I regret the thongs, but we can't have you jumping off again, can we?'

Della stared down at the rawhide thongs that lashed her wrists to the seat rail of the wagon. The tender flesh was beginning to chafe. Although bruised and dishevelled as a result of having jumped from the speeding vehicle earlier, she was calm and contemptuous as she studied the strip of tortured volcanic rock they were passing through.

'You can't keep me tied up for ever,' she said above the smash of wheels.

'We're not talking for ever,' he stated coldly, glancing back. 'Just for as long as it takes to know we're in the clear, is all.' He arched an eyebrow at her. He'd been briefly obsessed with this woman but that was already in the past. Her only value to him now was as a hostage, the most valuable one he could have chosen, he believed.

'They'll get you,' she promised fiercely. 'The sheriff won't allow you to escape, nor Shannon.'

That hit home. His face twisted. 'Your taste is all in your mouth, Della baby. And you must be really desperate to be relying on a cheap gun butcher like that to help you.'

'Shannon only shot Stack because you sent him to murder him.'

'I wanted the bastard dead because of the way you looked at him!' Wylder shot back involuntarily. Then he clamped his mouth tight and slapped the horses hard. 'Waste of a good man as it turned out – you empty-headed little bitch!'

Silence fell between them. Despite all her bravado, Della was afraid. She had retired happy last evening, thinking of Shannon. By dawn she was fifteen miles from Buffalo Horn in the company of the man who'd abducted her from her home after robbing the bank and murdering two men. She'd heard the faint stutter of guns backtrail once during their flight, now the only sounds were those of hoofs and wheels carrying her further and further away from him... It was at that moment she sighted the horseman. It was only a momentary glimpse of a mounted figure far off amongst the ugly bluffs ahead. The rider was quickly gone, but she knew her eyes weren't playing tricks. She glanced at Wylder. Plainly he'd seen nothing, being fully occupied with the driving. Berg and Hancock, bringing up the rear, were blinded by the dust.

She felt a quick kick of hope. Shannon!

she thought, her gaze sweeping the way ahead desperately now. A minute passed before a second horseman flitted swiftly between the outcroppings. Perhaps it wasn't Shannon after all, possibly a posse which had somehow managed to overtake and get up ahead?

'What are you staring at?' Wylder barked.

Alarmed, she forced a brilliant smile and began chatting to the man animatedly, all smiles and dimples, desperate to keep him occupied.

A half-mile rolled by, the sun now blasting down. Hancock and Berg were slumping in their saddles but Wylder plied the whip with vigor, miraculously restored to good spirits by Della's flattering attention. A narrow-walled pass loomed directly ahead and the teamers plunged into it, welcoming the sudden shade.

Then came the shot.

It was close, shockingly loud, and even Della knew it was a heavy rifle. There was another sound blending with the rifle echoes and she realized it was Berg, screaming. Twisting, she saw the little man tumbled headlong from his saddle as the walls of the pass rose higher on either side and abruptly the confined space was instantly transformed into an inferno of gunshots and screams, plunging horses and hoarse shouts, the pungent stink of cordite – a maze of terror.

Wylder had his sixgun out as the teamers reared high on their hind legs, hoofs boxing the air. The man fought to bring the animals under control as leaden hornets howled all about him. Suddenly the off-wheeler crashed dead in the harness, crimson spraying high. Mad-eyed, the second teamer lurched wildly back against the thorough-braces, the force jolting the vehicle sideways onto two wheels where it teetered before coming down on its side with a mighty crash. Wylder was flung high and wide while Della was held securely against the upended seat by her bonds.

Three of the steel-handled black crates

remained enmeshed in the wreckage but the fourth had shot out to strike a boulder with shattering force, bursting apart at one corner.

The crate bled bright yellow.

Hancock's mount had gone down in that first murderous volley. Unhurt, the big man sprang clear of the animal, shooting wildly until a fierce-eyed figure with a mane of red-gold hair showed above the high walls, triggering twin sixguns in one continuous rolling roar to smash the outlaw down in a welter of crimson, dead before he struck ground.

Wylder couldn't believe he was able to make it to his feet and dart back to find cover behind the wreckage without being cut to ribbons. A startled Bannerman couldn't believe he had failed to account for the tall man either – until realizing moments later that Houston and Blazer had quit their secure ambush positions to go hooting and hollering down the steep slopes, less like hardcase killers now, more like boys at a school picnic.

Their eyes were on that gold.

For weeks and months the Bannerman gang had lived like dogs and dreamed of the big one. Suddenly, now that it was here before them, real and tangible and not just empty owlhoot dreaming, all discipline and restraint was abandoned.

Nate Wylder was now a man alone as he crouched behind the shattered luggage-box of the overturned wagon as Bannerman exploded from cover to come leaping down the steeply sloping wall, red with rage. Blasting wildly and screaming curses at his henchman, the outlaw made a fearsome sight, yet one which offered Wylder a desperate last chance. Suddenly he had three exposed targets.

His .45 roared instantly and Houston, who'd reached the floor of the pass, kept rushing right past the gold crate with a sudden third eye in his forehead until he crashed into the wreckage and fell backwards, never to move again.

Instantly Blazer realized his exposed

position and dived desperately for rock cover as Bannerman ploughed to a halt on the trail and cut loose at Wylder's position. As the air again whistled with lead about him, Wylder ducked low to catch a glimpse of Chav Cody showing himself for the first time, fifty feet above. His first shot was good and the badman came crashing down end over end in a spectacular fall that held Wylder's attention a moment too long.

Bannerman made it to the far end of the wagon and almost cut him in two with a fierce volley that felled him like a butchered steer.

In an instant the silence came crashing down and Della, sprawled against the leather seat, stifled a sob at the horror of it all as the two surviving badmen traded looks then slowly circled the wreck to stare at both the dead and the gold.

'We … we done it, Reece,' Blazer panted. 'We–'

'Shut up!' Bannerman was still enraged by how close they'd come to losing everything simply because Blazer and Cody had acted like fools. But suddenly, mesmerizingly, the spectacle before him was beginning to banish his wrath, and he was starting to smile as he took a step towards the broken case – then froze.

'Hold up, Reece!'

Both whirled. Shannon stood thirty yards away with a sixgun in his hand, hazed by drifting dust and smoke. Instantly Joe Blazer dropped into a crouch and was bringing his cutter up to firing level when Shannon's Colt belched once and slammed him lifeless on his back.

The smoking Colt swung on Bannerman. 'Don't do it, Reece,' the whispery voice said. 'You let me leave the other day, so I owe you one. You can horse it and get gone…'

'Don't do me any favors, kid.' Bannerman seemed to be expanding physically before the eyes of both the ashen-faced girl and a motionless Shannon. The guns in his fists were slowly lifting; he appeared in the grip of something stronger than himself. It might have been pride; it might have been a vanity too big for just one man. There was gold in his eyes, and total unforgiveness. 'You've Judased on me, boy, and you surely have to pay. It's only fittin'.'

'Don't make me do it, man!'

But Bannerman was already making his play, hands sweeping up with impossible speed. Shannon sprang sideways, the Navy Colt blurring. A bullet tore the heel off his boot and pain lanced his side as he struck ground. His finger jerked twice and scarlet gunflashes flared viciously to drive Bannerman back on his heels, caving in at the middle, unable to believe the massive weight of his smoking guns. He stared across at Shannon with faint surprise, then fell slowly to his knees and rolled forward on his face.

With his hand pressed against his side, Shannon rose and went to Della.

It was two days before Shannon was strong enough to travel. He recuperated in the suite at the Federation Hotel formerly occupied by Nate Wylder, the slug in his side having been removed by the town medico, and all nursing undertaken by Della.

Rory Honeysett, quite overcome by the recovery of his shipment, had insisted Shannon come to recuperate in his home. But having personally turned over his $100,000 worth of dust to the banker even before going calling on the doctor, Shannon had declined.

He'd told Della everything, beginning with the story of his harsh beginnings and lonesome drifter's life leading right up to his involvement with the Bannerman gang. She had the option of passing this information on to her father, the law, or both, but instead simply told him she loved him and wished just to be with him. Always.

By some miracle she seemed to understand his need to bury his past and live free – free of the outlaw trails, free of the thin-blooded men of the towns.

There was no need to convince her of his love. She'd known that from the beginning.

They drove away together in morning sunshine with Shannon's ugly roan tethered to the buggy and Della's trunks stacked high behind the spring seat.

Towners had gathered in groups to wave them off, the menfolk sadly realizing that early weekday mornings at Chinnick's would never be the same again, the womenfolk tearfully noting what a beautiful couple they made.

Her sisters wept, even though well aware that it would be far easier to find husbands now that Della would not be around to divert the eye of every potential suitor.

Even her father found solace in the midst of his sadness. A headstrong young woman like Della was a difficult burden for a respectable widower with a position to maintain.

Only Della's grandmother wept a truly unselfish tear when she waved down at them as they drove past the great house. The girl was doing exactly as she herself had done so long ago, riding away with a man all said would bring her grief, but who she knew would always be at her side. She was waving goodbye to Black Sean, the wild boy of her youth as they faded from her sight. To the man who had his spirit, and the girl who had his blood.

So Shannon and Della left, never to return, nor once doubting the beckoning life that lay ahead. They drove away from Buffalo Horn that day until they could no longer be seen … vanishing for ever into the timeless legends of the West.

The publishers hope that this book has given you enjoyable reading. Large Print Books are especially designed to be as easy to see and hold as possible. If you wish a complete list of our books please ask at your local library or write directly to:

Dales Large Print Books
Magna House, Long Preston,
Skipton, North Yorkshire.
BD23 4ND